FIC
RHODES

HARDSCRABBLE
VALLEY

HARDSCRABBLE VALLEY

•

James Rhodes

AVALON BOOKS
NEW YORK

PRINTED IN THE UNITED STATES OF AMERICA
ON ACID-FREE PAPER
BY HADDON CRAFTSMEN, BLOOMSBURG, PENNSYLVANIA

TO
Georgia Paxton & William G. Seif because they cared.

AND TO
Justin Jacobson, who likes my stories.

Chapter One

This begins the saga of Horace Featherbone—that's me. For whatever reason, I thought I would put pen to paper and make a record, or a diary, or whatever you might feel obliged to call it, of my life so far.

Born and reared in Weed Patch, Missouri, I came to adulthood at one inch short of the top of the doorway. I will be the first to admit that I am not the sort of man who would make Solomon edgy to be around. Cannot help that; I really try hard at ciphering and spelling but there's other things what I consider more urgent in life. Such as ropin' and ridin' and being as truth-telling as the day is long.

To get on with it, both Pap and Ma parted

company when I was three. So my rearing was up to my Uncle Looty and Aunt Millie Drue. They were both hardworking and honest to a fault. And I was greatly saddened when they met their ends when their house caught fire one evening when I was eighteen.

Later I learned it hadn't been an accident but a right deliberate fire set by Monk Hastings, a conniving, evil-as-sin layabout. He had pilfered Uncle Looty's savings then set fire to the house, with poor Uncle Looty and Aunt Millie tied to the bedposts. I made a vow over their graves that I would hunt Monk Hastings down and somehow avenge their parting.

With the house gone and all their savings stolen by Mark Hastings, I had no desire to stick around Weed Patch. I sold the land for a middling sum, saddled up, and rode westward. It didn't matter where I was headed; I just rode toward the setting sun.

Along the way I decided to stop at Loueena Barnloft's spread—or rather her pap's. Wanted to say good-bye and tell her I was on my way.

Loueena was at the pump looking as pretty as she could be. She was drawing well-water for the house and she dropped the bucket when she saw me coming.

"Drat you, Horace Featherbone," she cried out. "Now look what you done made me do."

"Didn't mean no harm," I said, leaning on the saddle horn.

"You always never mean harm. You know what you are, Horace Featherbone? You are hard luck on two long-stretch legs. Trouble always comes whenever you appear."

Now wasn't that sweet of Loueena? She can say something that sounds mean as a starved wolverine but she don't mean none of it. That's probably why I am going to miss her.

"What you hanging around here for anyhow?" Loueena said, dipping the bucket again for another try at water.

"Just came over to say good-bye," I answered. "I'm leaving Weed Patch."

"Where you bound for?"

"Don't know. Just riding west."

Loueena shrugged as she drew another bucket from the well. "Why now? Thought we was going to the square dance this Saturday night."

"Guess that's old news now. I'm leaving town. Will you miss me, Loueena Barnloft?"

Loueena made a kind of half-moon with the side of her lips, shrugged her pretty shoulders, then said, "Maybe. Just a little. Now I'll have to find someone else to take me to the square dance."

Those first words tugged at my heart, almost bringing tears to my eyes. But I had made up my mind and nothing, not even Loueena Barnloft's love, could make me change my mind.

"Guess I'll be on my way," I said, and reined my horse.

Loueena just picked up the bucket of water, waved one of her delicate hands, and said, "Have a nice trip."

I rode away, my heart heavy as a brook stone in my chest. It was only when I reached the summit and turned to look back that I saw Reuben Brodie come from around the back of the Barnloft house. Loueena ran to him and she hugged him like he wasn't a long-lost brother but someone much dearer to her heart.

I may be slow sometimes but I'm not totally stupid. Loueena Barnloft was gone from my mind as soon as I topped the next ridge and rode down the other side.

Besides, there was Monk Hastings to find and reckon with.

Chapter Two

Minutes, hours, and a few days went by as I rode my piebald from Missouri. Strapped to my saddle was the small chamois bag that held my money from the sale of my aunt and uncle's land.

Uncle Looty had given me a pistol for my seventeenth birthday and also a few instructions on how to handle it. He even tried to teach me how to use the weapon.

He put can after can on the split-rail fence that squeezed in his property, and had me aim and fire. Aim and fire. It was just a waste of valuable gunpowder. The earth beyond the fence grew foggy with the dirt I kicked up from all my valiant efforts.

"Tell you what, son," Uncle Looty finally said. "You best learn to be real quick with your lip because you sure ain't with a gun."

Other folks might find those words sorrowful to hear but to me they were a lesson. A good lesson on how to get on in life. Only thing was I really wasn't much good at jawin' either. Lord above knew I tried. Tongue-tied, that was me. Especially around the fairer sex, like Loueena Barnloft.

But Loueena was no longer my true love. She now belonged to one Reuben Brodie, a scalawag if ever there was one. Loueena, it seemed, had met her match in Reuben. From that moment on Loueena was wiped from the slate of my mind.

A few nights out of Weed Patch I had ridden long in the saddle and had decided to rest that night near an outcropping of small boulders on a hillside. I ate a cold supper of chilled beans and biscuits and took care of my piebald before hunkering down to rest these weary bones.

I was awakened at dawn by the sound of voices, loud voices. I got to my feet, shoved them into my boots, and waited.

"You are going to swing high from this tree, Zack Hockenbrew," one loud, crude voice yelled.

"I ain't Zack," came another voice. "That's my twin brother. I'm Hack. You got the wrong man."

"Twin brother," came a third voice, cold with hardness. "That's another of your lies, Zack Hockenbrew. Just like you lied about not taking that poker pot at the Gilded Lady."

"That was Zack, I'm telling you. He done took that money," cried the second man. "He's getting away with that money."

"Wrong man, my Cousin Effie," came the snarl from yet another man. "You 'fess up to it, Zack Hockenbrew."

I did some rapid reckoning and decided that Hack or Zack was in a river of trouble. Whatever the pitiful feller had done, he didn't deserve to come to his end with a rope tied around his neck and swinging from an oak tree limb.

Slowly I reached for the pistol Uncle Looty had given me. The early morning sunlight glinted off the barrel and I wrapped an old piece of kerchief around it for fear the men at the oak tree might catch me sneaking up on them.

"Better say your last words, Zack Hockenbrew," someone said, and there was a mean smile in his voice.

"I ain't Zack Hockenbrew, I tell you!" the condemned man pleaded. "Look at my right arm. Zack has a heart tattoo on that arm. I ain't got no tattoo."

"What does that matter?" a man said.

"Tattoos don't mean nothin', 'cept maybe some local fool wants to mutilate his body," another man spoke.

All this time I was creeping close to where the hanging was to take place. I'd seen one hanging back in Weed Patch and I didn't sleep good for a few days. Not that the man didn't deserve it; Loyal Colman had killed a man for no just cause. Maybe one day I'll get over this feeling about justice and hanging—after all, the Good Book says we ought to take an eye for an eye, or something like that.

Anyway, here I was, not minding my own business like I rightfully should. By all rights I should be fixing my biscuits and beans and brewing some strong cowboy coffee. This sure wasn't any of my affair.

Still, this jasper Zack, or Hack, kind of got to me and I hadn't even laid eyes on him yet. There was just something in his voice. Reminded me of a hound dog, Lizzie, I once had who could make an undertaker weep when she took to baying at the moon.

I figured there wasn't much time for me to dawdle. Yet I had no idea how I would come to the rescue of this poor, unfortunate critter.

As I peeped over the top of the hill I saw a tall, spreading oak tree. Over one of the reaching branches hung a rope with a hangman's noose at one end. It swayed eerily in the early morning breeze over a man, probably Hack or Zack Hockenbrew, whose hands were tied behind his back.

Grouped in front of Hack/Zack were three men. Four saddled horses were grazing nearby. One of the men walked over and grabbed the reins of one of the horses and led it back to where the doomed man was standing. He motioned to one of the men who helped sit the poor, unfortunate miscreant onto the saddle.

"Time's awasting," the man who had led the horse to Hack/Zack said.

To my way of thinking it was now or never. However, I hadn't any idea of what my mission was.

I felt the weight of Uncle Looty's pistol like a millstone in my hand. I glanced at the weapon instead of looking where I was putting one boot after another. This was a mistake. Somehow a wandering, water-searching root of the oak tree entangled itself around my foot.

I struggled for a moment and before I fell to earth my pistol went off, firing wildly into the morning's glow.

I don't exactly recollect what happened next because there was a scrambling noise and some shouts, then the sound of horses galloping away.

When I staggered to my feet I saw three horsemen headed away from the oak tree where poor Hack/Zack was to meet his untimely end. Only there was no Hack/Zack around. And the noose at the end of the hanging rope had been cut clean away. I was befuddled. What had happened to the noose? And where was Hack/Zack? His horse was still standing beneath the oak tree.

Now that the three hangmen had gone I felt free to show myself and I stood up to get a better view. As I rose to my full six-foot-four I saw a man lying on the ground. It had to be Hack/Zack.

Good heaven above, I thought with a shudder. *I've killed a man.* The very one I was aiming to rescue. Nobody will ever know how full of pain I was at that moment. Almost as sorrowful as when I lost my aunt and uncle. It wasn't going to be a good day for me.

The least I could do was to bury the miserable drover. That was what any decent killer would do, regardless of the fact that the shooting death had been an accident. I shuddered again as I looked around for somewhere to plant Hack/Zack's body.

As I stood there, pity oozing like sap from a maple tree, I heard a moaning sound. At first I wasn't sure it wasn't the wind in the tall grass. Then I heard it again. It was coming from the fallen body of Hack/Zack as he sat upright and held his head between his hands.

I strolled over to where he sat rubbing his head. He glanced up at me and then at Uncle Looty's pistol.

"Good shooting, Sure Shot," Hack/Zack said. "Saved my life. I owe you one."

"What did I do?" I asked in all honesty.

"Such modesty," Hack/Zack managed a rough, gargled laugh. "You set them three a-ridin' and you shot that rope clean through at the knot. Never seen such shootin'."

"It was an accident," I pleaded.

Hack/Zack laughed and staggered to his feet. "Sure. I believe you. Anyhoo, we'd better hit the trail before those three find out I'm not swayin' in the breeze." He felt his head once more. "Must have cracked it on a rock when I fell."

Hack/Zack saying we ought to vamoose held a lot of wisdom. In a half hour the two of us were well beyond the hanging tree and headed far from the three hangmen. It was then I reached over and rolled up Hack/Zack's right sleeve. His arm was bare except for a spattering of freckles and plain dirt.

"So you *are* Hack," I said.

"That's the holy truth," Hack said.

"And you do have a twin brother named Zack."

"May I be struck from above if I'm not telling the truth."

I couldn't help but notice Hack's body shifting slightly in the saddle as he said these words.

I'm not one to meddle into a person's private life so I didn't ask Hack about why the three men were so bent on stretching him with a high rope.

Didn't need to. Hack Hockenbrew, it turned out, was a glib and able talker.

"Zack and me was born and reared on a spread in Montana. Zack was always the reckless, loco one. Always getting into trouble with the law. Once he even tried holding up a stagecoach out of Cheyenne. Only the man riding shotgun was quicker on the draw than Zack.

He clean shot the Colt right out of of Zack's hand without disturbing a pinch of flesh.

"Zack went to jail for a year or two and it was there he got the heart tattoo on his right arm. When he was released he and I hit the trail. There were plenty of scrapes along the way but I managed to get Zack out of all of them. Then we landed in Careless City. Here Zack got into a poker game and made off with the pot at gunpoint.

"Since I was a spittin' image of Zack the three gamblers mistook me for my brother. That's how come you almost saw me dancing in the breeze with a noose for a necktie."

It sounded right honest to me and there was pity in me for the poor, misunderstood, mistaken man.

"Where you bound for, Hack?" I asked when he'd ended his woebegone saga.

"Any place but Careless City," was Hack's reply. "What about you, Horace?"

"No place in particular, just ramblin'," was my answer.

"Mind if I ramble with you?"

"Suit yourself."

"Then let's be at it."

We hadn't rambled too far when we spotted

three men on horseback out toward the horizon. Hack was the first one to spot them.

"It's them!" he shouted. "They've come to finish the job."

I looked frantically around for a place for us to hide. Not too far away was a stand of trees. They'd make a perfect place to see and not be seen.

"Over there," I said and spurred my piebald into a gallop with Hack right beside me. In a few minutes we were safely hidden from view. I wasn't too happy about this development. Don't recall any time in my life when I ever ran from trouble. Didn't cater much to the feeling.

Hack, on the other hand, seemed to relish the idea that we had bamboozled the men. I was beginning to have serious doubts about my traveling companion. Then I drew myself up sharply. Here was a poor, innocent man who had nearly been hanged for a crime he had no part in. *For shame,* I chided myself. *Where is your Christian charity?*

I found Hack Hockenbrew to be a very agreeable traveling companion. He not only let me tend his horse when we camped for the night but ate my vittles with no complaining at all. Like I said, a most amiable companion.

As we stretched out before the campfire one night, resting our heads on our saddles, Hack asked me about myself. He seemed genuinely interested in my life story, especially when I told him of the money I carried in the sheep-skin bag hinged to my saddle.

When it grew late and the campfire was noth-ing but softly glowing embers, I fell asleep. It had been a long and tiring day. All had ended well and I was at peace with the world. Even my dreams were peaceful except for a moment when I thought or dreamed someone touched and moved my saddle. Just a tad bit. When I woke up the morning sun split my eyes and I blinked at the glare.

The fire had gone out and there was nothing but gray ashes now. I scratched myself and ran a hand through my fur-brown hair then glanced over to see if Hack was awake.

He not only was awake but gone.

I sat up and called out his name. No answer. Then I saw his horse was missing. His saddle was still where he had flung it last night. I couldn't figure out what had happened to him.

Maybe those three scalawags bent on hang-ing Hack had caught up with him during the night and had done away with him. It must have been what had happened. They had strapped him to his horse and ridden away with poor Hack.

I decided right then and there I would track them down, even before breakfast.

I reached for my saddle, picked it up, and went to my piebald. As I was cinching the saddle I saw with disbelief that my chamois bag filled with the money from the farm was missing. I left my horse and rushed back to where I had laid my head during the night, thinking the bag must have come loose and I had dropped it. I looked around, hardly bothering to breathe. It was nowhere to be found.

Slowly I came to the reckoning that Hack Hockenbrew had made off with my poke. There could be no other explanation.

Once again my green was beginning to show. I had trusted this man from the very first time I had met him. I was a poor judge of character. I had let his quick tongue lead me into a trap. A trap that had cost me dearly.

Or maybe not!

If Hack hadn't taken his saddle, perhaps his riding bareback might not be as swift as if he rode in a saddle. I didn't know that much about the man. At the moment his behavior was such a sad disappointment to me. I had trusted the man, really believed in him and his plight in life. How much he had confided in me was true, I had no way of knowing. One thing I did know, the man was a thief.

I am not a tracker; still, I could see for a short span the hoofprints of his horse. They led away from camp and toward the high bank of the river we had settled on during the night.

The river was a fierce, angry one. Even from the distance we had camped we could hear it tearing at the high bluff and screaming over the bed of rocks. It was a mean, roaring torrent; woe betide anyone who dared to cross its surface or swim its vile waters.

Ahead of me I could see far down the bank of the torrent. So far away as to be a mere speck, I thought I saw movement. I urged my horse to a full gallop in order to catch up with whoever it was. If the rider was not Hack maybe whoever it was might have run into that miserable scamp.

All the way down the top of the bluff I kept thinking about how I had been duped. I couldn't really have helped what I had done. Uncle Looty had talked over and over to me about the trust one must place in his fellow man. He was so good at this that I found myself, many times, looking for the good in men when, in some cases, there was none to be found. Hack Hockenbrew namely was one of these.

Wrapped, as I was, in my "pitiful me" thinking, I was almost taken by surprise when I came upon Hack Hockenbrew.

His horse had become lame for some reason and Hack was about to go by boots alone across the wide, reaching prairie.

"Hold on there!" I shouted, and Hack almost leaped out of his foul-smelling store-boughts. "You got something of mine and I want it back—now!"

Hack began backing away from me. I drew my pistol, not intending on using it, but to show the thief I meant business.

"Now, hold on there," Hack said, stepping slowly backward, both hands lifted high toward the heavens.

"I want my money," I said. "The money you stole from me. And I want it right now, hear?"

Reaching cautiously with one hand, while the other touched the sky, Hack brought out my sheepskin and tossed it toward me. In doing so he became unbalanced as the earth beneath his feet gave out a sudden rumble and then gave way, carrying Hack along with it, into the rushing, churning water below.

I tried to reach Hack and save him but he

instantly disappeared into the torrent. I saw him bob once above the foaming water before he vanished forever, headed downstream.

There was nothing I could do so I tended the sore horse and, along with my piebald, headed back to the campsite. I was still in a daze over what had happened to Hack Hockenbrew. A little sad at his parting, but maybe hanging wasn't to be his destiny.

Chapter Three

It was, in truth, a most dismal night when I made camp again, and the flickering flames of the dying fire did very little to lift my already somber mood.

Lying back on my saddle I gazed heavenward at the scattering of stars that all seemed as lonely and forgotten as myself. Although I had only known Hack Hockbenbrew for a brief spell, I had gotten to a sort of friendship with him. He truthfully wasn't the most savory person in this troubling world, but at least he was someone to jaw with.

I do not recollect how long I lay there by the campfire, just as pitiable and miserable as any motherless critter could be. Then I decided

21

it would do me no earthly good to dwell on the past and I took one last pull on my cup of coffee before tossing the remains onto the fire. There was a hissing sound and a spire of smoke drifted into the night air. I closed my eyes.

Whatever it was, either footfall or the crackle of one last burning ember, woke me. I sat up like a shot and reached for my Uncle Looty's weapon. Someone was standing still as a statue in the shadows.

"Hark!" I shouted. "Come out of there so I can see plainly who you are. And come out real slowly."

The creature moved slowly toward the almost dead fire. I, by this time, had gotten to my feet and the weapon was at the ready. The man, for indeed that was who this interruption was, finally came close and the faint light cast by the dying fire brought out his features. I gasped. I seemed to tremble all over and the weapon in my hand had turned to heavy stone.

"You . . . you . . ." I could barely speak from the sight before me. "It can't be. It just can't be."

The man finally spoke. "Didn't mean to

scare the skin off you. Just wondered if you could spare some grub and a cup of coffee."

The man looked like Hack Hockenbrew, was built like Hack Hockenbrew, but he didn't sound like him. Maybe he still had some of that river water in his lungs.

"Back from the dead, that's what you are. Back from the dead." I had finally regained my voice.

"Me? Naw, I ain't no ghost. Maybe I look like one with all this trail dust on me. But, naw, I ain't no spirit. Name's Zack, Zack Hockenbrew. What's your handle?"

I told him in a voice that sounded like it had come from some deep, dark cavern.

" 'Bout that grub? I ain't had nothin' to eat for two days. I ain't got much money but I'll be pleased to work for my supper."

That didn't sound to me like Hack Hockenbrew speaking. Still, the resemblance between this Zack and Hack was uncanny.

"I can feed you," I said. "First I got to prove something to myself. Roll up your sleeve on your right arm."

Zack didn't appear to be in the least surprised at my request. "Want to see the tattoo, do you? Ain't nothing fancy. Matter of fact

I've been thinking of having the durn fool thing taken off."

With that Zack rolled up his trail-stained shirt sleeve, revealing the tattoo. It was of a heart with the words *Mona, I love you* in the center of the heart.

"Who was Mona?" I asked, not remembering you just didn't pry into another's background out here in the wide-open country. Secrets had just better be kept that way. There was trouble aplenty without inviting it in.

Zack didn't seem to mind my asking and he told me it was a lady friend he had once met in a saloon in some town in Montana. She would be forgotten long before the tattoo would fade from Zack's arm.

While Zack related to me the short but interesting story of his brief encounter with Mona, I went about fixing him some food. As Zack told the story of the tattoo he squatted by the fire and I relaxed enough to put aside Uncle Looty's weapon.

"Hack, my brother, was always the ladies' man. He was quick-tongued and right glib when it came to charming the ladies. Only this time it was Mona who took to me instead of Hack. He rightly got real angry and did his best to humiliate me in front of the fair woman. Didn't work. Mona just turned her back on Hack and turned them sky-blue eyes on me."

It was interesting, I mean the story was interesting, the way Zack Hockenbrew related it. And I settled back to let him ramble on.

"Well, time came for the two of us, Hack and me, to move on. Because of Hack's temper and his not-quite-honest dealings with folks, we never stayed in one place too long. The night before we left I had my arm tattooed so's I could remember the first true love of my life."

It was a sad story that would have touched the heart of even the coldest undertaker.

"Then we came to this new town. Hack got into a poker game, cheated, and ran away with some of the stakes. All I can recall is seeing him riding slick-bent for leather out of town with three men chasing him. Saw all this from our hotel window. Never saw Hack since then. You ever seen my brother on the trail? I know you called me by his handle."

It was then I had to tell the poor man of the sad fate of his twin brother. It was one of the most difficult things I ever had to do. But Zack took it well.

"Stupid man, standing on the edge of the

bluff like that. Bet he'll bob up somewhere out in the Gulf of Mexico. Then he'll start all over again trying to cheat people out of their pokes. If he ever got a decent job and put his cunning to work he'd make something of himself."

That was the last Zack spoke of his twin that night. Since it was getting late I allowed him to spend the night, seeing's how he had so recently been struck by mourning of his deceased brother.

Surprisingly I slept well that night and awoke to see Zack up and about, starting a fire and already brewing some coffee. So unlike his brother was he that I grew to liking the man.

"How did you get here?" I asked. "Don't see any horse, except mine and your brother Hack's."

Zack pointed to his well-worn boots. "Shanks mare. Hack sold my pony behind my back so's he could get some gambling money."

Again it was a sad, pitiable story and I was obliged to hand over to Zack his brother's horse. After all, it did belong to the Hockenbrew family.

"Mighty thoughtful of you," Zack said. "I'll remember your kindness. And I'll pay you back by allowing myself to ride alongside you. That's if you are in agreement."

Couldn't think of any reason why Zack shouldn't, so I just nodded.

After we had eaten our biscuits and slab bacon and drank our fill of coffee we kicked dirt on the low-burning fire, saddled up, and rode away.

Unlike his brother, Zack turned out to be an honest and reliable trail partner. It was easy to jaw with him and he had stories to tell me that furthered my education of life and all its pitfalls and possibilities.

We rode by day in that year of 1885 and ate and slept by night. Along the way Zack brought food to our table by trapping small animals and birds on the wing. There were always fresh, clear-watered streams to slake our thirst and we rarely, if ever, encountered anyone on the trail.

Rarely, I said, but there are always exceptions to every rule. I recall one day, getting on to dusk, Zack and I had found a likely spot to call our campsite. We had washed up in the running stream and I was fixing some meat Zack had brung down that afternoon.

As we sat around the fire and chomped on the meat and biscuits, a lone rider approached.

There was something about the rider that didn't raise the hackles on either Zack's or my neck.

Drawing near so we could get a better look, he was just a boy, or had that look of someone quite youthful. And he was polite. Something in his favor.

"Evenin', men. Couldn't beg a meal from you this night, could I? Been a long, hard ride today."

"Sure thing," I said. "Tether your horse over there next to ours. You can wash up at the stream. There's plenty for all of us."

"Much obliged," the boy said, and did as he was instructed.

"Nice young 'un," Zack said, scooping up vittles for the stranger.

He was thankful, and as I said, polite, and accepted the food, which he consumed heartily. He was not given to much jawing but listened quietly to what Zack had to say about some of his wanderings.

When we were finished the boy insisted on cleaning our plates in the stream and making sure all of them were spotless before bringing them back.

I offered to let him spend the night but he declined.

"Got some traveling to do this night," he said. "Right nice of you to share what you had with me. Maybe I'll see you, Horace and Zack, on the trail one of these days."

Before he could ride off Zack said, "Never did get your handle. In case we meet up again."

The boy touched the brim of his hat and said, "I'm Bonney. William Bonney. You'll probably be hearing of me one of these days."

With that William Bonney rode off into the night.

"Let's get some shut-eye," Zack said.

"Good idea. Hope that William Bonney don't get into any trouble."

"Nice kid like that?" Zack said. "No way."

On our fifth day on the move, Zack and I saw a herd of cattle on the horizon and we urged our horses in that direction. They were not moving but grazing on the fine, green grass that sprang from the rich soil.

As we approached we neared one of the drovers who touched the brim of his Stetson in a welcoming way.

"Howdy," he said. "Lookin' for work?"

"Always," Zack was quick to reply.

"Sure could use a job," I said, and the man

smiled at me. I guess because of my height in the saddle I look more experienced than I really am.

"Ever done any cookin'?" the drover asked.

"One summer my uncle let me cook for a herd that was passing through our town on the way East."

"Good enough. Cookie left us yesterday. Got in a quarrel with one of the drovers. The chuck wagon's back there."

The drover, who it turned out was the trail boss and called Wes Boone, told us everything we needed was in the chuck wagon and all we had to do was shout if we lacked anything.

Zack was real excited that we had found employment. He was quick to learn about pots and pans and what went into them.

By the time the evening meal came we had come up with some vittles that brought hungry looks from the drovers as they came to eat.

Most of the men were good-natured and easy-going. They kidded each other about what had happened out there on the range. Then they joshed me and Zack about our cooking.

"Is that buffalo still kicking inside the pot?"

"I wonder what's in this stew? I heard something rattle."

"Coffee could make a cougar cry. Just the way I like it."

Zack and I took the joshin' because the drovers actually cleaned up their plates and stuck them out for seconds and even thirds.

Wes Boone came by and took it all in. "Guess I done chose right, huh, boys?" he said, meaning us. There was agreement all around.

Every one of them was pleased with the offering. All except one by the name of Joshua Judd. J.J., as the drovers called him, was the first in line and the last to bring us his plate for washing.

"Them others might like your vittles but I think your cookin' is fit only for the hogs."

At first I took it that J.J. was just joshin' Zack and me like the rest of the drovers. How wrong I was.

It was Zack who told me later that he had learned from the other drovers that J.J. was a troublemaker. He had been the one who had caused the last cook to up and leave without collecting his pay.

"There's a bad apple on every tree," Zack said to me. "Stay clear of that one, Horace. He'll bring us nothin' but trouble."

I always try to give someone a second chance. That's how I was reared. In this case it was a big mistake as far as Joshua Judd was concerned.

He always had a bad word for me and my cooking. I just could not please the drover. Went out of my way to make sure he got a good helping on his plate.

It did no good.

One time he deliberately pulled his plate back as I was dishing out some stew. Instead of it falling to the ground as he had planned, it slopped all over his pants legs.

"You stupid, clumsy son-of-a-crossed-eyed-skunk!" he yelped in anger and pain.

Now, I don't mind someone sullying me or my habits but when it came to calling my mother a cross-eyed-skunk, that was too much. I slammed the ladle down, reached across the table, and grabbed J.J. by the collar. He was caught off-guard and I shook him until his chin kept dancing off his chest. Then, with one mighty burst of energy, I flung him to the ground.

The other drovers let it be known that what I had just done was fine to their code of behavior. J.J. got to his feet, wiped the stew from his pants, then turned to walk away. Before he left he turned, gave me a mean look, then said,

"You'll be sorry you done that, Cookie. You'll be real sorry."

"Don't let J.J. bother you none," the other drovers said as they got their suppers.

"He's just a lot of wind. Always has been a troublemaker."

When I cooled down I was sorry I had let my temper best me. I am a peace-loving man, taught so by my kind and church-going Uncle Looty.

After Zack and I had cleaned up I started to walk away.

"Where you headed?"

"Going to find J.J. and make my amends."

"Don't do it. It will just worsen things. Leave that man alone. He's a mean one."

"Maybe so, but I think I should at least try to let him know there's no hard feelings."

Zack shook his head. "Don't know how you've lasted this long these many years. Still, I guess you've got to live your life the way you see fit."

I went to find J.J., who was bunking down for the night. When he saw me coming the scowl on his face was like an animal getting ready to spring.

I extended my hand and said, "No hard feelings?"

J.J. just looked at me for a moment before he spat on the ground and turned his back on me.

"Just remember what I said. You'll be sorry, you and that good-for-nothing friend of yours. I'll get even. You can count on it."

There was nothing more I could say. The poor, unhappy creature just couldn't be friendly. I truly felt sympathy for the drover as I went back to the chuck wagon and put away the pots and pans Zack had scoured for the morning breakfast.

"So what happened?"

"The man is a sad, miserable, and ornery soul. Feel sorry for the pitiful creature."

"Sorry!" Zack moaned. "He's worse than a polecat and I wouldn't trust him any farther than I can heave my horse."

Even so I always try to be around good-hearted, kindly folk. It's better all around that way.

Sleep didn't come easy that night. When I did finally drift off I had nightmares and bad dreams. When I awoke I vaguely recollected that someone was after me and that a heavy black cloud was chasing me all over the waste-land. Out of the cloud stepped Joshua Judd who had grown four heads and six arms. In the hand of each arm was a weapon of some kind. A gun, a knife, an ax—things like that. It took a long while for me to shake off that nightmare.

When I told Zack about it he just said, "Better watch what you eat before crawling into your blanket for the night. I kinda thought the meat had a gamy taste last night."

Probably right. I wasn't one to linger over bad tidings, indigestion, or bad dreams. Besides, that day Wes Boone had said I could ride with the herd while Zack brought up the side with the chuck wagon.

I was nervous and very excited to ride alongside the huge mass of cattle. The day was fair with just a little breeze and the sun couldn't have been warmer.

This was the life I had dreamed of back in Weed Patch as I was growing up. I could listen for hours to old drovers spinning tales of their adventures riding drag, flank, or swing alongside a cattle herd.

To me I was at the peak of my youthful experience. Nothing could ever compare with the feelings I had as I rode alongside the herd.

Then it happened.

I wasn't sure how but I recollect that I heard a loud popping noise and the herd suddenly bolted. I was confused and bewildered by the stampeding cattle and choking on the dust spewed up by their galloping hooves.

All I could do was gallop alongside the herd, hoping that I wasn't getting in the way. It was a terrifying experience and I wondered if perhaps I might have chosen the wrong work to get hooked up with.

The herd raced blindly ahead and all the drovers were doing their best to try and calm the animals down. I did what I thought was best from where I rode and kept any strays from roaming too far from the herd.

It was all over in a matter of minutes and the other drovers moved among the herd soothing them with soft, sweet words. I followed their lead and was surprised at the effect it had on the wild-eyed beasts.

Once the herd was settled and back to foraging on the grass, I saw J.J. and Wes Boone headed in my direction.

Expecting some sort of praise for my actions in this first-time stampede, I was stunned when Wes Boone said, "Pack up and get moving. And take that friend of yours with you."

I saw a sly smile on J.J.'s lips and I wondered what he found so amusing.

"Why, Mr. Boone?" I asked after the stun

had worn off. "What did I do wrong? It's the food, isn't it? Too much pepper? I'll watch that."

Wes Boone shook his head. "The cooking ain't what's wrong. Got no trouble with that. It's what happened just a while ago."

"You mean the stampede? I tried my best to keep the strays from leaving the herd."

"J.J. here tells me you were the one what caused the stampede. Can't have someone like you riding with the remuda."

"Me? I didn't do anything. I was just riding along like you told me to do."

Wes Boone wasn't a happy trail boss at that moment. Something was bothering him and he seemed almost regretful that he had fired me.

"You and Zack be gone by sundown," Wes said. "We'll find outselves another cook, somehow."

Before he rode away he turned to me and said in the most sincere voice, "Sorry, Horace. Real sorry."

With that Wes Boone rode away followed by Joshua Judd, who glanced over his shoulder. The sly look on his face told me that the varmit was actually pleased Zack and I had been asked to ride on.

With a heart as sad and low as the bottom

of a dry well, I rode back to where Zack was waiting with the chuck wagon.

"You look like you've just lost your best friend," Zack said, and that was not too far from the truth. Only it wasn't a friend I had lost but work that I thought I could enjoy.

"No use getting those pots out," I said. "We won't be using them."

"You gone loco? What we gonna cook with? The palms of our hands?"

Then I had to tell him. Zack's mouth hung open like the outside of the biggest cavern in Arizona.

"You tellin' the truth? We've been fired? And I'll bet I know who's behind it. That Joshua Judd. He'd do anything to get you fired."

"Maybe so. But that's all in the past. We'd better get packing."

"I don't understand it. I heard the noise you was telling me about. That crackling, popping noise. Right before the stampede. Something ain't right here."

We started to pack. Both our horses were tethered nearby. Zack and I didn't have much to stow since we traveled light.

As we were cinching up our saddles Wes Boone and J.J. and some of the drovers rode up. It was Wes who dismounted and came over to where Zack and I were standing. Slowly I saw J.J. ease out of his saddle, that snake-like grin still cuting like a slash across his ugly face.

"Can't let you two leave without your pay," Wes said. He reached inside his pocket. "I owe both of you some wages."

"We can use it," Zack said. He was not in the least shy when it came to worldly gains.

"Where you headed?" Wes said as he counted out some bills.

"No place in particular," I said. "We haven't made any plans."

The other drovers had gotten off their horses by now and had formed a half-circle around the four of us. I could see by their faces they were not cheerful about what was happening.

"I'd like to keep you on," Wes said. "Best cooks we've ever had. And the men like you too."

Zack sent a mean look at J.J. "Not all of them. There's one bad apple that's been spoil-ing the whole bunch for some time now."

J.J. acted as if he had no knowledge of whom Zack spoke. He appeared to be as in-nocent as an angel from beyond.

Wes handed us both our pay and J.J. started

to climb back in his saddle. As he did a small, bright-colored packet slid from beneath the saddle and fell to the ground. J.J. didn't seem to be aware of it.

Bearing no grudge, I walked over and picked up the packet. "Here, J.J., you dropped this," I said as kindly and well-meaning as I could.

J.J. started to reach for the packet but Zack was a little too nimble for him.

"Give me that," J.J. shouted from his perch on his saddle. "Ain't no concern of yours."

"Well, now, looky here," Zack said, holding up the packet. "Hmm, Little Red Devils. Now what do you reckon a feller like J.J. would be doing with these?" Zack examined the packet closely. "And it's been opened. Looks like some of these little firecrackers have been used."

The drovers moved closer to J.J. and Wes Boone walked over to Zack.

"Anybody hear a noise just before them cattle ran loco?" Zack said, looking around.

All of the drovers agreed and moved even closer. "That's the noise I heard just before the stampede," I spoke up.

"What you got to say for yourself, J.J.?" Wes said as he took the packet of firecrackers from Zack. "You told me it was Horace who caused the stampede. You lied to me."

J.J. looked like a rat that had been cornered in a round house. He suddenly spurred his horse and galloped away.

"Want us to catch him, Boss?" One of the drovers shouted.

Wes shook his head. "He won't be back. And he won't be seen around these parts ever again."

"Guess we'd better be on our way," I said to Zack. "Sorry about the stampede, Boss. Guess J.J. didn't know what he was doing."

"He knew," Wes said. "Just like he knew when he drove the other cook away. I had my suspicions then. Should have quick-booted him right then. What'll it take besides my regrets at your leaving to make you and Zack stay on?"

I looked at Zack. He nodded.

"We'd better get to rattling these pots and pans or you drovers won't be eating nothing but canned beans tonight," I said.

That was all anybody needed and Wes and the drovers went back to the cattle. Zack and I had our work to do and we still had our jobs.

"Can't help feeling sort of sorry for J.J.," I said, reaching for a ladle.

"Sorry for that ornery whelp? Save it, Horace, he got just what was coming to him."

Guess so, but I don't rightly like to think bad of anyone. Even a skunk like Joshua Judd. I often wondered in my travels whatever became of the man until one time outside of Big Hawk City, I happened to be wanderin' through Boot Hill and I saw a wooden marker that read, JOSHUA JUDD, KILLED IN A GUNFIGHT. R.I.P. I certainly hoped so.

Life on the range for Zack and me was good living after J.J. had departed. I even got to ride, now and then, with the other drovers. I got along good with them and they seemed to accept me as one of their own. Zack was content to stay with the chuck wagon and smoke his pipe.

In a few weeks we neared our destination, and the thought of a good bath and clean clothes and somebody else's cooking was something to look forward to.

Still, off and on, especially when the night closed around and there was only me and Zack, Monk Hastings always came back to me. I knew him, had seen him around Weed Patch, so his face was burned into my head. "Someday, Monk Hastings, someday," I would say before sleep came to me.

Chapter Four

New Paris wasn't exactly new nor did it resemble Paris, or so I was told. It was where we unloaded the cattle for them to be shipped to Chicago or wherever the cattle ended up.

After Wes Boone paid Zack and me, we got us a room at New Paris's best hotel and got rid of the trail dust we had packed away all those many months. When we had both cleaned up and put on new duds we went downstairs to the dining room.

We both had never seen such elegant words on a menu. The waiter, who had a mustache that could spear a whale, did some explaining for us. We settled, finally, for steak and potatoes and some fresh vegetables. The vegetables

43

brought me back to Weed Patch 'cause that was my aunt's pride and joy, her garden directly behind the family house.

After we had done away with the food, Zack headed for a saloon to do a little gambling. Since I had no interest in bottled spirits I took a stroll downtown.

There really wasn't much to see of New Paris and I found that the main street was only four blocks long. I did find a barber shop that gave me a good haircut and a smooth shave. The barber took a liking to me and let me take one of the magazines that he kept for customers waiting their turn in the chair.

I tucked the magazine beneath my arm and walked once again down the street. I found a wooden bench, shaded from above by an overhang. Sprawling on the bench, I began to turn the pages of the magazine which was all about farm equipment and mostly advertising. It was not a magazine I would have chosen, but it was free.

I scanned the pages with the ads and was amazed at what people were listing for sale: rocking chairs, used saddles, dress spurs, baby clothes, and what have you.

As I turned the page I heard some music coming from the distance. The kind of music

I once heard back in Weed Patch the day the circus came to town. I got to my feet.

Coming down the dusty street was a red, yellow, and pink calliope on wheels. The whistle-like music was perky and brought all the townsfolk out to see and listen. Trailing the calliope was an elephant with his trainer beside him and behind them a caged tiger who paced back and forth, now and then growling at anyone who ventured too near his cage.

The parade stopped right in front of where I was standing. Then I saw the reason why. One of the wheels on the calliope had come loose and was wavering back and forth like it was going to fall off. The girl playing the calliope was beginning to tilt to one side and was in danger of falling off.

I dashed to her rescue and arrived surely in the nick of time. She slid from behind the calliope and right into my outstretched arms.

"Love a duckling!" she muttered as she gazed up at me. "You saved my life. Now, put me down."

I am always an obliging person and I gently lowered the girl to the dusty street.

"Where are we anyway?" she asked, dusting herself off.

"New Paris, I think," I replied.

"Just my luck, never the old Paris, just the new one. Story of my life."

At that moment a tall, skinny man with a long, pointed chin came rushing up.

"Cristobel, are you all right?"

"Yes, thanks to this young man. He saved my life."

The man stuck out his hand and I clasped it in mine. "I'm Lawton Lonzini—kind of rhymes with zucchini," he said with a twinkle in his eye. "I own this circus and if there is anything I can do to repay you for saving my high-wire madonna let me know."

"Horace Featherbone, sir. It was a privilege to be of service. Only happy that I was able to help."

"This is, as I said, my prize high-wire attraction, Cristobel Columbus."

Cristobel again favored me with one of her dazzling smiles. "Horace, that ain't really my name. It's Mildred Pfung. Mr. Lonzini changed it for the show. Are you coming to see us? It'll be this afternoon. You could be my guest on account of you being so nice and all."

"Cristobel!" a thunderous voice bellowed from behind the calliope. "Where are you?"

"Out here, Gunther. I'm all right."

Around the calliope came a tall-as-me man with a scar on his face that snaked down from his forehead to his lower lip. He strode boldly over to where me, Cristobel, and Lawton were standing.

"This here's Horace—he saved my life. I was falling off the calliope and he caught me. Wasn't that brave of him?"

Gunther looked as though he didn't think anything I could ever do would be brave enough. "Let's get that wheel fixed. I'll need some help."

"Be willing to do that," I volunteered.

Gunther shrugged and said, "Offer accepted."

It didn't take Gunther and me very long to right the calliope, and he hoisted Cristobel up where she belonged.

"Let's get moving," Gunther said as he vanished behind the calliope.

"Who is Gunther?" I asked Lawton. "And what does he do?"

"He swallows swords," Lawton said. "And he finds me roustabouts when I need them."

"What's a roustabout?"

"A fancy name for a handyman, a jack-of-all-trades. Puts up the big tent and takes it down and handles the cats and the other animals."

"I'd sure like to have a job like that," I said wistfully.

Lawton looked me over and said, "You out of work, son?"

"No, I'm with the herd that came through this morning. But I'd quit that job in a wink if I could be a roustabout."

Lawton extended his hand. "Then you got a job. My roustabouts all stayed over in the last town we played in. Been looking for someone to fill their shoes. Don't know of another feller to help out, do you? The wages is good."

Zack came rushing into my mind. He, like me, always was eager for adventure. What more adventurous life could there be than joining a circus? A dream come true.

"I got just the man for you, Mr. Lonzini."

"Meet us just south of town. That's where we're going to put on the show. And call me Lawton, Horace."

"Yes, sir, Lawton. Zack and I will be there, you can count on us."

The calliope began its music and the parade continued past me. I didn't stay to see the clowns or the rest of the performers. I was in a hurry to find Zack.

He had said he was going to a saloon to do some card playing. I had noticed that there were three such establishments in New Paris. The first two gave me no comfort since Zack was not there. Besides, the tobacco smoke and the stale smell of spirits was sickening to me.

In the last bar I had better luck. Zack was just coming through the bat-wing doors as I reached the saloon.

"This town is unlucky for me," were his first words. "I didn't have a winning hand all day. Unlucky is what this town is."

"No it isn't," I said. "This could be your luckiest day."

"The sun's got to you."

"We got ourselves another job. I know you'll like it better than cooking."

Zack seemed interested. Highly interested. "Tell me about it. What kind of a job is it?"

"Hear that music?"

"A calliope, so what."

"Doesn't that music do something to you, Zack? Doesn't it make you want to kick up your boots and get your blood to pounding?"

"Sometimes. Right now a good steak and taters could do the same thing. Why you so het-up about that music?"

"We could be hearing it all day long. We could be hearing it while we work."

Zack's eyebrows crawled up his forehead. "You got us a job with a circus? Is that what you're jawing about?"

I couldn't hold back our good fortune any longer. "That's right, Zack. You and me, we're going to be roustabouts."

Zack put his finger to the side of his jaw, a gesture I was well aware of. A gesture that meant he was in deep-down thought.

"What are we waiting for? Let's roustabout."

First thing we had to do was tell Wes Boone of our good fortune and our new positions.

Wes was in the hotel lobby sitting in a plush chair stretching his legs and puffing on a cheroot. He looked so at ease and relaxed I almost hated to tell him about our decision. Still, it was only fair and something that in all honesty had to be done.

I had decided to be as diplomatic and tactful as I possibly could. When Zack and I stood before him I said, "Howdy there, Mr. Boone. Zack and me are going to join the circus. Won't be cooking anymore. Thought you should know."

Wes Boone almost swallowed his cheroot.

He must have been that overcome with good wishes for the both of us.

"You are both plum loco," he said.

What a sense of humor that man had. He didn't want to show his true feelings so he decided to josh with us.

"All the best of luck finding a new cook," Zack said.

"You'll be back," Wes said. "You ain't cut out to be circus folk. When you do, the jobs are still open for both of you."

I swallowed real hard. Mr. Boone was doing his best not to break down.

"Well, we best be on our way."

"Be seein' you," Mr. Boone said and took a big puff on his cheroot and leaned back to count the squares on the overhead ceiling.

Zack and I hurried to our room and gathered up what miserly possessions we had, then paid for our room, left the key, and headed south of town.

When we got there we took care of our horses and went in search of Lawton Lonzini. We found him with two other men he had found in New Paris to help out.

"Good to see you, Horace. I'd hoped you wouldn't disappoint me. Who's your friend?"

I introduced Zack and they shook friendly

hands. Then Lawton gave us orders for working. Zack and me and the other two men set to work putting up the big tent. It might have seemed like cruel labor to the other two men but Zack and I were having the time of our lives. I tried to cheer up the other two men but they only shook their heads and said, "This is just a job to us two. When we get our pay it's off to Abilene for us. You are just plain loco if you are getting any fun out of this."

Zack and I ignored them after that. Too bad they couldn't see the excitement of being this close to circus folks. It took a while to get the tent and the ring set up but when we were done Cristobel came by.

"Why, Horace, you done a fine job. I hope you stay with the circus for a long, long time."

I thanked Cristobel for her kind words and made her acquainted with Zack, who fell under her spell just as I had. But just as what had happened earlier that day, Gunther came by and whisked Crisobel away.

"He's a jealous one," Zack said. "Hope we're not running into another Joshua Judd here."

"He's just making sure Cristobel is properly protected," I said, because I wanted to get off on a good footing here in the circus world.

After Zack and I had done our work on the tent Lawton came over to thank us. He was a most thoughtful and considerate man and one I would follow even into the direst battle.

"Take a rest, go get something to wet your tonsils, then meet me where the animals are kept."

"Thanks, Lawton," I said.

Zack and I found a stand where there was lemonade aplenty. We got our cups filled and took seats under the shade of the canvas canopy. There were two clowns sitting on the next bench and they greeted us warmly.

"Here's a flower for you," one of the clowns said, handing me a long-stemmed rose. As soon as I took it the rose seemed to come alive and leaped back into the clown's hand. Everybody laughed because I must have had a real surprised look on my face. Then I caught on. The rose was on a long rubber band. I had to laugh at my surprised reaction.

"You are all right," the clown said, this time handing me a bag of peanuts that didn't bounce back to him. The two clowns came over and sat with Zack and me.

"What kind of work you been in?" one of the clowns asked Zack and me.

"We were with a cattle drive," Zack said. "Horace and I ran the chuck wagon."

Both clowns were impressed. "Gee," the one who had given me the rose said, "I'd like that kind of life. Free to ride and be your own boss."

"Nothing like it," Zack said. "Only Horace and me, we like to try different things."

"That's right," I said. "Always wanted to join up with a circus. Have wanted to all my life."

"So here you are," the second clown said. "You got your wish."

The other clown, the one with the rose, looked me over and then said, "You a roustabout?"

"Sure thing."

"You should be up there." He pointed skyward. "Like Cristobel. I'm not a waging man but I think you'd make a great flyer."

"What's that?" I asked.

"Trapeze. Swinging out over the crowd, doing somersaults in the air and having someone catch you before you fall."

"I don't know about that," I said.

"Why not?" Zack said. "You're a circus man now. Got to try everything. Maybe someday you'll get your chance."

I did not know then how prophetic Zack's words were.

After we finished our lemonade Zack and me said good-bye to the clowns and went in search of the animals. When we found them, sure enough, there stood Lawton waiting for us.

He took Zack and me around to see the tigers and lions and the three elephants. He explained real carefully what and how much they ate and drank.

"That will be part of your job, the care and feeding of these critters," Lawton said.

It was not work for either of us since we both had soft feelings for animals. It wasn't long before we got the hang of it and in a few days the animals seemed to recognize us and greet us when we came to feed and play with them.

I found it particularly enjoyable since Cristobel now and then drifted by to speak to Zack and me and to encourage us. The only wasp in the syrup was that Gunther was never far out of Cristobel's sight. He never ceased coming around just when Cristobel was telling Zack and me something of interest about life in a circus.

Cristobel was obedient and always went

away with Gunther even though the look in her eye seemed to say that she would rather be with Zack and me.

The circus folded its tent one evening and we were off to another city. Zack and I rode with the animals which was all right with the both of us. I was never happier in my life as we rolled along to another destination.

Each town or city we played in, it was up to Zack and me to find routabouts. We would scour the street in search of men who were in need of work. We always managed to find plenty of helpers eager for a day's pay.

I grew very fond of the folks in the circus and made a lot of friends.

Cristobel sometimes came to where Zack and me were working, only to be led away by Gunther.

What I reckon to be my most special moment of the day was watching Cristobel practicing on the high-wire. There were times, I must confess, that my heart leaped into my throat when she appeared to lose her balance, because she worked without a net. Somehow Cristobel never toppled from the wire, always catching her balance before she fell.

One day, after Zack and me had finished watering and feeding the animals, I was watching the trapeze folk perform. This particular feat of derring-do captivated me and I stood fencepost-still watching them fly through the air only to be caught by one of their troupe who swayed back and forth, head down and legs hooked to the trapeze.

After they had ended their practice, Angelino, the leader of the group, came over to me. "Mario is leaving the troupe," he said sadly. "He misses Italy and is homesick."

"I'm sorry," I said. "Mario is a good man. I will miss him.

"We need someone to take Mario's place," Angelino said.

"Sure hope you find someone," I said as helpfully as I could. I did not want the trapeze group to have to give up because Mario got homesick.

"I think I already have."

"That's good, real good. Did you have to look very far?"

Angelino shook his head. Then he reached out and put a strong hand on my shoulder. "Not far at all. You will replace Mario. With a little practice, of course."

"Now, hold on just a minute there," I protested. Although I had this jittery feeling inside that told me something great was about to happen to me. "I don't know nothing about that trapeze or swinging through the air like a bird. The only time I was ever in the air like that was when I used to swing by a rope over a swimmin' hole."

"You'll learn. After all, you will have the best teacher—me."

"When do I start?"

"Tomorrow morning at eight o'clock. Don't be late. You'll do fine, just fine. Do not worry."

I could hardly wait to tell Zack about what had happened. He was sitting on an old tree stump smoking his pipe when I found him.

"You look like you're about to burst your gullet," Zack said when I walked up to him almost out of breath.

"I'm going to be a flyer, Zack!" I cried out. "Just like you said I would be. Mario's out and it looks like I am in. What do you think about that?"

Zack blew a perfect smoke ring into the air.

"Just make sure the drover on the trapeze catches you and doesn't have slippery hands."

So it was settled. Zack had given me his blessings and his worldly-wise advice. I was too excited to get much sleep that night and so I went for a walk and talked to the lion and tiger and whispered of my good fortune in an elephant's ear.

Finally I did manage to fall asleep and when Zack pounded on my pillow the next morning I almost leaped out of bed.

As I was hurrying to practice I happened to meet Cristobel.

"Horace, I just heard the news. I think it's just great that you will be there on the trapeze. It's a whole different sort of world while you are up there. Everybody looks so small down below. You are going to feel good about it."

"I already do. Thanks, Cristobel, for those helpful words."

Cristobel was going to say something else when she glanced around and, seeing Gunther, said, "Got to go, Horace. Take care up there."

Those were some of the dearest, sweetest words anyone had ever spoken to me. Cristobel was the most thoughtful, kindest person in the whole circus and I always will remember her being so helpful to someone as green as I was.

I watched Cristobel hurry to Gunther, who looked kind of ugly at me and didn't return my friendly, neighborly wave to him.

When I got to where the flyers were rehearsing, Angelino was waiting for me. It is really beyond my pitiful vocabulary to write down my woeful first day on the trapeze. By the time rehearsal was over I was ready to turn tail and head out of town. I felt so low that I could hardly look any of the other members of the troupe in the face.

"Not to worry, Horace," Angelino said. "For a first day you were very good. Every one of us had to have a beginning. Tomorrow, tomorrow you will do better. Believe me, I know of what I speak."

Well, those were uplifting words and I went to find Zack and help with the animals. Anywhere that I could feel I was doing a good day's labor.

Even Zack was understanding and that night he even put liniment on my sorry, aching body.

"Guess I don't have to tell you to sleep well," Zack said. "You'll do that right well tonight for sure."

He was right, as usual, and I did fall asleep soon after I stretched out prone on my cot. I don't remember dreaming or anything else until the sun cracked my eyes at dawn.

Surprisingly Zack's liniment rubdown had done its work. I found my muscles were hardly aching and I was raring to get to feeding and watering the animals.

By the time we finished Zack came along with me to watch me work out with the troupe. It was a marvel of some kind but I didn't make nearly as many mistakes as I'd made yesterday. Angelino was very giving with praise.

"A few more days, Horace, a few more days," he said. "You'll fly through the air like an eagle."

I wasn't exactly certain I had any bird-like qualities. Nevertheless it was uplifting to hear such praise and flattery. Even Zack patted me on the back and said encouragingly, "At least you didn't break your neck." He had always been an encouragement to me.

A few lessons later Cristobel showed up. She sat below and I could hardly keep my mind on what I was doing. Still, when a break came, she was full of good, cheering words and made me feel better than I knew I really was.

Of course, as usual, that didn't last long, nor did Cristobel last any longer. Gunther, skulking in the background, came over to lead her away. I wasn't disappointed that he held no uplifting words for me. But before he left, with Cristobel out of earshot, he said, "If I owned this broken-down circus you would be the first to go. Understand?"

Something told me that Gunther and I could never be friends and share the same plate of food, as the saying goes. Why, I'll never know, because I treated him with great respect and consideration. If I had to make a guess I suppose it had something to do with the fact that I was taller than he and I never once volunteered to watch his sword-swallowing act. It just wasn't something I would take pleasure in viewing. Nothing else came to mind.

Day by day, hour by hour, and performance by performance, I became a little more sure of myself on the trapeze. The other members of the troupe became as close as kin to me. Zack joined in with us and was taken to their bosom and accepted as family.

It was during an afternoon performance in a town in New Mexico that I had an uneasy feeling. I cannot put it into words but there was something in the air that was unsettling.

That morning Lawton had met with me and Zack while we were tending the animals. He seemed a little different from his usual open-hearted self.

"Anything wrong, Lawton?" I asked as I fed a chunk of beef to the lion.

"Can't put a finger on it," Lawton answered. "You know something, Horace, if someone would give me a fair offer on the circus I'd take it. No questions asked."

This did come as a sweeping surprise to me since ever since I had met Lawton Lonzini he was all for the circus life. He was always enthusiastic about the different acts and always had a smile on his face. That smile was gone today.

"Do you mean that, Lawton? I always thought you would be with the circus until its last days."

"Can't explain it. Guess I'm getting too old for this traveling from town to town. After a while they all sort of look alike."

These were worrisome words coming from the lips of Lawton Lonzini.

I would think about them as the day grew on.

It was later, when I jawed with one of the clowns, that the trouble started at the entrance to the big tent. About fifteen ruffians from the town had tried to get in for the performance without paying. The ticket seller tried to stop them but the ruffians overpowered him and beat him senseless, leaving him at the entrance to the big tent.

Inside, the word had gotten out to the roustabouts and the members of the circus. A great fight broke out while I was on the trapeze. I looked down and saw townsfolk and their children scurrying to get away from the melee caused by the rowdies.

Without waiting I quickly grabbed a rope and hand-over-hand slid down to the ground. In the distance I saw Zack trying to hold off two of the ruffians and I raced to his defense.

I grabbed one of the boys by the collar, spun him around, then lifted him above my head and flung him into the group who were bent on tearing up the tent. Then Zack finished off his lone attacker and the two of us dashed over to battle the other troublemakers.

One of the men had an ax handle and was starting to club one of the clowns. A stream of blood soaked the clown's white makeup and gave him an eerie appearance.

I grabbed the handle before the man could inflict another brutal blow. I used it on the ruffian who ran from the tent holding his head. One of the rowdies caught me from the side and stunned me slightly. However, as I said, only slightly, enough to make me angry. This he shouldn't have done. Being a peaceable man by nature and taught by Uncle Looty to withdraw rather than pursue, I was slow to anger. But this cowardly attack made me see red and I whirled around and with a crashing blow sent him sprawling out of the tent.

Aroused to wrath now, I joined Zack and the roustabouts and the clowns and we soon had the ruffians running for their lives. They leaped on their horses and spurred them into full gallop.

After they had gone Zack and me and some of the others tried to assess the damage. Over in one corner I saw the body of somebody who had been felled during the row. I hurried over and helped Lawton Lonzini to his feet. As far as I could tell there was no blood or signs of serious damage done to the elderly man.

"Just got the wind kicked out of me," Lawton said. "I'll be all right. You go back to help the others, Horace. Has anybody seen Gunther?"

Until then I hadn't seen or thought about the burly sword-swallower. Now I glanced around and he was nowhere to be seen.

"If he shows up send him to my office, Horace," Lawton said. "Will you do that?"

"Most obliged to, Lawton," I answered.

Lawton limped out of the tent then and headed for his office. I went back to help the others right what had been overturned or repair what had been broken.

As I was busy with some overturned seats, Gunther walked by. He was looking around at what damage there was. When he saw me he said, "You cause any of this?"

By this time my anger was spent and all I said to Gunther, in the most civil of tones, was, "Mr. Lonzini wants to see you . . . in his office."

Gunther's scowling jowl changed into an almost pleasant grin, almost like the kind you see on a reptile's face. He didn't bother to thank me, just turned and almost ran out of the tent.

After that I was so busy working at repairing the damage done to the inside of the tent I didn't even notice when Lawton and Gunther returned. Suddenly there was a loud voice coming from either Lawton or Gunther, and me and Zack and the others switched our attention to the corner where Lawton and Gunther were standing.

"I have an announcement to make," Lawton said, and I seemed to feel a sense of sadness and weariness in his voice. "As of today the ownership of the circus will no longer be mine but rather Gunther's. He has made me an offer too generous for me to refuse."

The silence was like being hit by a falling

boulder. All of us workers just stood there. No words or curses or anything sprang from our lips.

"I hope that all of you will work as diligently for Gunther as you did for me," Lawton continued. "If not, I will be in my office for an hour to give you your well-earned pay."

Gunther said nothing all the while Lawton spoke but I couldn't help but notice the way he was glaring mockingly in my direction. I knew then that my days with Lawton's circus were numbered.

Now that Lawton had finished he sadly walked out of the tent and back to what was once his office. There was not one sound from any of the workers. They were still in a kind of shocked state, losing Lawton like that.

Gunther put his hands on his hips and in a loud, bragging voice shouted, "I'm the new owner now. Back to work, all of you. And I want this mess cleaned up in an hour. We got a performance tonight."

I glanced over at Zack, who shook his head like he could not believe what was going on. One by one the other workers went back to work.

I heard one of the clowns say to a roustabout, "If I didn't need the money I would pack up my satchel and tell this circus adios."

The roustabout just made a face and went back to work. Zack walked over and stood next to me.

"So what do we do now? I know there ain't a lot of love between you and our new owner. You aimin' to go to the office and see Lawton?"

Before I could answer, Gunther came boastfully over to the two of us.

"You can keep on working, Zack," he said. "But I want our trapeze man out of here as soon as he can get his belongings together."

"That must mean you are firing me," I said, and Gunther just grinned.

"I once told you what I would do if I ever became owner of this outfit. Now it has happened and I don't have a change of heart."

"How could you have a change since you never had a heart in the first place?" Zack said.

Gunther came at Zack but changed his mind when he saw that he would have to take on two instead of one. He cleared his throat and his face got as red as a blacksmith's new horseshoe.

"You git, along with your friend, Hockenbrew," he spurted. "You are fired. As of this here very second you are fired."

"Sorry," Zack came back. "You can't fire someone who has already quit. I wouldn't work for this circus one more minute now that you are the owner."

Gunther looked like he would explode as he turned and walked out of the tent. As soon as he was gone the whole bunch of men all shouted and clapped their hands.

"That's telling him, Zack," one of the roust-abouts said.

"I'm right behind you two," said one of the clowns. "There are a lot of other circuses where I can do my act."

I turned to Zack. "Let's get packed and go see Lawton. Time to move on."

"I am right beside you, Horace," Zack said in one of those rare times when he called me by my first name.

The clown trailed us as we walked out of the tent and parted company when Zack and I went to pack our belongings. It didn't take us long and after everything was sturdy and tight we hitched them to our horses' saddles and rode over to Lawton's office.

Lawton was there with Cristobel who had

been weeping. My heart went out to her because she seemed so alone and so frail.

"Heard what Gunther did to you two," Lawton said. "I am real sorry about that."

"Don't grieve none, Lawton," I said. "It's about time for Zack and me to be riding on. Got a lot of things and places yet to see."

Even though I tried to be gallant and noble and all those sort of fancy words, I was inside very sad of heart. I had always wanted to work in a circus, ever since I was a tadpole. My only consolation was that I had at least been able to see that dream be real even if it was just for a short stretch.

"Here's your wages," Lawton said. "I put a little extra in because you two were a couple of the best routabouts I ever had the pleasure of working with."

These words set real well with both Zack and me and I told Lawton that he was, indeed, a fine, honorable boss. Then I looked at Cristobel. "Hope those tears are not for anything hurtful to you, Cristobel."

She shook her head. "No, it's just that I too will be leaving the circus. And I want to leave as soon as possible."

"Nothing holding you here, is there, Cristobel?" Zack boldly asked.

Before she could answer the door to the office was flung open. Standing in the framework with his legs firmly planted was Gunther.

"There you are!" he growled at Cristobel. "I've been looking all over the place for you. C'mon."

For once Cristobel stood her ground—a pleasure to see, to be sure.

"No, Gunther. No more. I am leaving the circus. I am returning to Denver. You cannot stop me."

"We'll see about that. You are talking real stage-talk now. Been with the circus too long." Gunther swaggered menacingly toward Cristobel.

As he reached for her arm I once again felt the surge of anger rise within me. This, I'll admit, is not an admirable quality to be admitted in any worthwhile soul. Still, I'd had just about enough of Gunther and his rough treatment of sweet Cristobel.

"Take your hand off her," I said in as even a voice as I could muster. "I will not allow you to mistreat Cristobel ever again."

Gunther whirled and glared at me. "Or you'll do what?"

He did not get the last word out before I slammed my clenched fist against his jawline.

There was a loud crack of bone in the air and Gunther slid silently down until he lay prone on the floor of the office.

"Let's get out of here," Zack said with all his worldly wisdom.

"Good idea," Lawton said as he gathered up his portmanteau and took Cristobel by the arm. As Zack and I followed them out of the office I saw that Gunther hadn't moved from where he had fallen. I reached down and shifted his head to one side so that he would breathe easier and not suffocate. After all, that was the least kindly thing I could do for the varmint.

Once outside, the four of us rode away from the circus grounds, never once glancing back at the past.

When we had gone about two hours Lawton raised his hand to let us know that we needed to cease our riding.

"Here is where Cristobel and I must leave you, Horace and Zack. The trail we will travel will lead us to Denver."

"Thank you, both of you," Cristobel said. "I just hope that you both have successful travels. I am anxious to return home. There are my folks and a certain young man I am anxious to see again."

Zack and I wished them well and we sat on

our horses for a spell while Lawton and Cristobel rode away toward Denver.

"And us?" Zack finally asked. "Where to?"

"That way," I pointed in another direction
from Lawton and Cristobel. "Let's see what
lies ahead."

Maybe I'd meet up with Monk Hastings.
Even with all the adventures of the cattle drive,
the circus, and my short-lived trapeze career,
I'd never lost my focus. I'd settle my score
with Monk Hastings one day soon—or I'd die
trying.

Chapter Five

After Cristobel and Lawton had ridden away and Zack and I had gone another direction, I felt a hurt inside at losing such a special friend. I did hope that Cristobel would find happiness in Denver since she only knew misery while Gunther was in her life.

The land we rode through was hilly and we had to make our way carefully. Neither Zack nor I spoke much. I guess both of us, in our way, missed the circus life. It had been good to the both of us. There had been one wasp in the salve and that was Gunther, but he had gotten his just reward for his treatment of Cristobel. I couldn't help but wonder who this young man was she was so anxious to see in

75

Denver. I just hoped that he respected and cared for her far more than Gunther had.

Topping a hill, Zack and I suddenly found ouselves staring into the muzzles of three deadly-looking shotguns. Glancing up from the muzzles, I saw three ornery, dirty-faced men with eyes so mean-looking they would scare a grizzly.

"You are trespassing on Weezle land," one of the men said. "Ma gave us orders to shoot to kill any trespassers."

"We didn't know this was private land," Zack said. But the middle man drew an even sharper bead on him.

"Don't matter," the third man said. "There are signs posted."

"We didn't see any signs," I said. "We're sorry. We meant no harm."

The first coyote glanced at the other two and said, "Shall we kill 'em now?"

The middle man cocked his head thoughtfully for a moment then said, "Naw. We best take 'em to Ma. She'll know what to do with them."

The third man nodded. "Yup, Ma said to bring 'em to her before we done 'em in."

Before Zack and I could protest, the three men—we later learned they were brothers:

Lem, Bert, and Handy Weezle—urged us on by cocking their shotguns and taking a nervous aim at Zack and me. Maybe Ma Weezle might have told the boys to bring strangers to her, but there could always be accidents. We meekly rode with the Weezle boys.

We didn't have far to ride, for over another hill stood the Weezle ranch. Even from this distance I could tell it had not only seen better days but even those days hadn't been so glory-filled.

The boys directed us to a hitching rail where they took the reins and tethered our horses.

Before us the ranch spread out like a wide, long, deadly insect waiting to devour whoever came too close. It was not a pretty sight. As I gazed at Zack I felt certain he was of the same opinion.

Two mangy, gnarly hounds crept out from beneath the wooden porch and showed grimy, green fangs as they growled at Zack and me.

"Git," said Lem, and kicked blinding dust at the hounds, who retreated to their lair still growling and snarling in their wickedness.

"Inside," Bert said, nudging me with his weapon.

"You too," Handy told Zack, who managed

to give his tormentor a hard, get-even-someday look.

We stopped at the door, which was clawed and splintered either from the weather or some unearthly hand, as it was creakingly opened and a blowsy wraith appeared before us.

"Whatcha got there, boys?" croaked the wraith as she opened the door a little ways more.

"These two we caught trespassing," Bert said.

"That's right, Ma," said Bert.

"Want we should do 'em in now, Ma?" asked Handy, a little too eagerly.

Ma Weezle made a hitched-up look on her face as she leaned forward to get a better view of Zack and me with her demon-red eyes. "Naw, not yet. Got some plans for these two. They're both too young and pretty for my idee. Bring 'em on in the house."

With shotguns poking us in the back, Zack and me entered the pit of vipers. Surprisingly the inside of the ranch was neat and dusted and smelled of pine soap. There were a few well-upholstered chairs and couches tossed about and a huge, mahogany desk with a stained-glass lamp sitting on top of it. But the one piece of furniture in the place that surprised me was a grand piano all polished and shiny as a brand-new coin.

"Sit!" Ma shouted at me and Zack. "You boys stand over in the corner. Keep your eyes on these two to make sure they don't try and get away."

The boys obeyed Ma instantly and were on guard. Me and Zack sat down on one of the couches. Ma Weezle eased her gaunt frame into a chair directly away from us.

For at least five minutes Ma Weezle just sat there staring at Zack and me. I didn't see her or her three sons blink once in all that time.

Then Ma smiled a lumpy smile at us and said, "What's your handles, boys? Just your first names will do fine."

"I'm Horace," I said. "And this here is my good friend Zack."

That was all Ma Weezle asked of us and that was all the information I gave. Ma chewed on this for another brief spell, then she said, "You fellers much on matchmaking?"

It was such a surprise to both Zack and myself that all we could do in reply to Ma's question was just shake our heads.

"I tell you something." Ma got up from her chair and walked over to the piano. She picked up a picture in a gilded frame and brought it back with her. All the way across the room she hugged the picture to her bosom like it was something priceless like silver or gold.

When she took her seat in her chair once more she turned the picture so Zack and I could see plainly that it was of a man and woman dressed in their wedding garb. I couldn't be certain but the woman might have been Ma Weezle.

"This here is my late-departed husband Orville," Ma said.

"Amen!" the Weezle brothers whispered in awed unison.

"He was the dearest thing to my heart. And he built this here mansion by hisself. With the help of the young'uns, of course."

"Yes, ma'am," the chorus came from the brothers Weezle.

"Orville was taken to his reward a few years ago. Brought to an early grave one day when he went to slop the hogs. Poor Orville lost his footing and fell among the hogs. He didn't stand a chance. When we found him all we had to bury him with was his overalls and his polka-dot bandana."

There was a sob in unison from the Weezle brothers, and Ma sniffed twice.

"You wonderin' what all this has to do with you two?"

I nodded, not having the gumption to speak.

"It's simple. You and your friend go to Spitville and find me a groom. If you do, you are free as the breeze."

There was an ominous silence. "And if we don't?" I ventured.

The answer was the deadly sound of the clicking of three shotguns from the Weezle brothers.

I turned to Zack. "What do you say, Zack?"

"Time's a-wastin'. Let's find a groom for this fair lady."

Ma Weezle didn't take to Zack's flattery. "Best be gettin' on with your chore. Spitville ain't that far away."

I would have asked Ma Weezle why she didn't have one of her sons pick a groom or why she herself hadn't done the honors. Then I thought better of it because I was anxious to get out of this place and away from the Weezles. As soon as we were away, Zack and I would ride till sundown without looking back.

That hope was splintered when Ma Weezle said, "Lem, Bert, and Handy will be watching you in town. Just to make certain you don't try to make a run for it."

"Oh, we won't do anything like that," I said.

"Just to be sure," Ma said. "Boys, get their guns. If they do a decent job, then give them back."

"If not?" Zack asked.

"Then my boys will have some mighty pretty souvenirs."

We five left Ma alone with her memories. Outside the hounds growled and snarled at Zack and me as we walked to our horses. Lem, Bert, and Handy leaped into their saddles and kept their shotguns at the ready.

They did not have to bother. Zack and me were not about to try and ride away. Not only were we afraid that the Weezle brothers were crackerjack marksmen, but we didn't know the way to escape.

Zack and me never said a word after leaving the ranch but I could almost read his thoughts. Like me, he was wondering how we could find a groom for the less-than-lovely, older-than-dirt Ma Weezle and just what sort of man was she seeking. Neither one of us had the faintest idea. We sat in a sad gloom wondering how we could get out of this terrible mess. No weapons, no idea where we were. No chance of finding a groom for Ma Weezle. Things looked worse than hopeless for us.

Far off in the distance I saw what appeared to be a town. Spitville lay dead ahead. The name made my mouth dry and I wondered how the town got its name. Only I had no desire to ask Lem, Bert, or Handy that question.

We rode on and each minute grew bleaker and bleaker. There seemed no hope for this impossible situation.

Arriving in Spitville, I saw one dusty main street with wooden buildings on either side. Few townsfolk walked the wooden boardwalk, and those that did glanced nervously in our direction. I suppose they were curious at seeing strangers like Zack and me in town.

We rode past several saloons with tinny music blaring forth from over the top of the batwing doors. An occasional drover stepped out, took one look in our direction, then turned on his boot heel to either go back inside or hurry down the boardwalk.

When we reached the end of the main street the Weezle brothers reined in their horses and dismounted. We did the same.

Handy took the reins of my horse while Bert took Zack's. "These you get back when you done found the right suitor for Ma," Lem said, and he and his brothers led our horses away.

Now that they were gone I said to Zack, "What are we going to do?"

"We could high-tail it out of town and make tracks on foot."

I shook my head. "We wouldn't stand a chance. These Weezles would be on us in a wink. And this time I don't think they would hesitate to use their shotguns for a little traget practice."

"Guess you're right. I don't think I've ever been in such a mess. And me and Hack have been in quite a few."

This was one of the first times since his brother's death that Zack had mentioned Hack.

We decided to take a stroll down through Spitville and maybe an idea might come to us. As we walked I glanced around to see if the Weezle brothers were anywhere to be seen. Even though I did not see them I felt their eyes were watching our every move.

Just ahead, on our left, was a barber shop.

"If there are any single men in this town, Zack, they might hang out in that place."

"Right on that one," Zack said. "Let's have a look-see."

Which we did. Inside, the one barber chair was occupied and the barber was busy clipping away. He nodded to us in a friendly way and said, "Have a seat, gents. Got a few heads ahead of you."

Zack and me looked at the six chairs and saw that three of them were taken. We took our seats and I looked at Zack and he said, "Now or never."

To the barber I said, "Ever hear of the Weezle ranch?"

At the mention of the name the barber stopped clipping away and all heads turned upon Zack and me. "I see you have. That makes it easier. You see, Zack and me . . . well, we've been asked . . . well, maybe not exactly asked but we promised to look for a suitor for Ma Weezle. If any of you is single—"

At the mention of Ma Weezle all the men sitting in the chairs got to their feet, grabbed their Stetsons, and rushed out of the shop. That included the man in the barber's chair.

When they had all gone the barber said, "Now look what you've gone and done. There goes all my customers."

"Sorry," I said. "All I did was mention Ma Weezle."

"That was enough. You two must not be from around these parts."

"We're not," I said.

"A word of advice. If you want to stay

healthy and plan on sticking around these parts, never mention the name Weezle in this town."

"That bad, huh?" Zack said.

The barber shook the few hairs he had trimmed off his last customer from the towel he had used around his neck. "Not a good idea. Let's put it that way."

"Thanks for the advice," I said. "C'mon, Zack we got our work cut out for us in Spitville."

As we started to leave the barber said, "Don't need a haircut, do you?"

We shook our heads as we went outside, no better off than when we had gone in. We leaned against the wall of the barber shop and slowly let our gaze drift up and down the street of Spitville. Word must have traveled fast because there was hardly a man seen either on the street or on the boardwalk.

"This is getting serious," Zack said.

"If we don't find someone for Ma Weezle you know what that means."

"Don't remind me."

I let out a big sigh and then said, "Won't do us any good just standing around. Let's get moving."

If we passed anyone while Zack and me

walked down the street of Spitville they either looked the other way or nervously walked faster. The name Weezle was hardly highly regarded in this small town. And after what had happened to Zack and me—the misfortune of straying on Weezle private land—I could understand why.

"I wonder if we could buy or rent horses at the livery stable," Zack asked. "If we could we might ride out of this mess."

"And who would be right behind us?"

"The Weezle brothers, I know."

By this time we were nearing one of the saloons. Even as far away as we were, we could hear loud voices in hepped-up arguments. The nearer we came the louder and rougher they became. Then there was a crashing and a smashing and two men tumbled out of the saloon, arms flailing and dust swirling in the air. Five more men staggered out of the saloon, egging the two men on. By this time we were almost in the middle of the fracas.

All at once someone fired shots into the air. Then we were all surrounded by the sheriff and his deputies. "Hold on—you men simmer down," the sheriff said. "I know you boys, you are with the Chapman gang. We'll all march nice and pretty over to the jail. If anyone gets out of line, deputies, shoot to kill."

A deputy shoved me and Zack, mistaking us for members of the Chapman gang—whoever they were.

"You are making a mistake," I said. "We don't belong with these men."

"Tell it to the judge," the deputy said. "Move on."

With the barrel of a gun aimed at both of us, Zack and me had no choice but to go along with the Chapman gang. This was the second time today me and Zack had faced the business end of a gun. Sure didn't seem like this was the best day of our lives.

Somehow the sheriff and his deputies got all of us into the crowded jail cell. The Chapman gang gathered in one tight circle. Me and Zack, outsiders that we were, found a corner of the cell which we shared with a man who had seen better days. His clothing was tattered and he hadn't had a haircut or a shave for days. And he looked as though he was not really certain where he was.

Since there was nothing much to do until Zack and me straightened things out with the sheriff, we began to talk to the poor, miserable unfortunate.

"Name's Bellows," the man mumbled, and there was a slight hissing sound mainly due to the slight gap between his two upper front teeth. "Adam Bellows. Awful crowded in here today. I been in jails where I was the sole occupant. Got waited on hand and foot then. Up in Cheyenne it was. Where you boys from?"

"Just passing through," I said. "I hail from Missouri. And my friend here is from Montana."

"Right happy to meet the both of you. Say you're called Horace? Like that name. And your friend is Zack—must be from Zachariah, am I right?"

Zack, who like me had taken a liking to Adam Bellows, agreed with our cell mate.

"Where's your family, Adam?" I asked. "Aren't they worried about you?"

Adam shook his head. "Ain't got one living relative. Just poor me against a cold and unfriendly world."

I reckoned that Adam's best friend was probably found in a bottle on the shelf behind a bar in a saloon. Then it hit me, just as it must have Zack, because we looked at each other at the same time.

"Adam, we got a friend we want you to

meet. When we get out of here, we'll take you to meet our friend."

"What kind of a friend?" Bert asked.

"A lady friend," Zack said. "You will like her, trust in us."

Adam seemed pleased that we were that interested in him. I couldn't believe our good luck. Of all places we wouldn't have looked, the cell of a jail was one of them. The more I talked with Adam the more I got to like the man. Zack was a great friend of the man himself.

When it came time for the sheriff to come around, the Chapman gang told him that we were not a part of the gang.

"We were just passing by, Sheriff," I said. "It was just a big mistake."

The sheriff thought it over for a moment or two then agreed that it had been an error on his part. "Anything I can do to make it up to you drovers, just say the word," the sheriff said.

This was our great chance. "There is one thing, Sheriff. Do you suppose you could let Adam Bellows out too? We'll take good care of him. We promise."

Again the sheriff took a moment or two and then said, "Why not. That cell's crowded enough as it is. Besides, Adam was only in here because he's a vagrant."

So the three of us thanked the sheriff and left the jailhouse.

Once outside Adam wanted to head for the nearest saloon. "Later, Adam," I said. "Right now we got to get you all spruced up for your lady friend."

"Oh, that's right," Adam said. "I almost forgot."

"Adam, you sit down there on the bench while Zack and I do a little jawing."

Adam just shrugged and plopped down on the bench. He looked indeed to be a most pathetic-looking sight. I wondered if Zack and I hadn't made a terrible, terrible mistake. But, on the other hand, what choice did we have? There was no other single male available in Spitville.

We still had our wages from the circus that we hadn't left with our horses. So I told Zack to go to the haberdasher's and buy some new duds for Adam. Nothing real expensive but not too cheap either.

"What about you? Where is Adam going to change into these new duds?"

"At the barber shop. I'll get the barber to give Adam a haircut and a shave and pay him to let us use his shop so Adam can change clothes."

Zack thought the whole idea was really workable. Then he looked at Adam sitting all forlorn on the bench. "Kinda hate to do this to the poor man. He seems like a real decent drover."

"I know. I feel bad about it too. Maybe Ma won't take to him and let us go for at least trying."

Zack cocked his head. "Ma might but I don't know about those boys of hers."

"Get going," I said. "I'll meet you at the barber shop."

Zack took off to find a haberdashery while I went over to Adam. I sat down next to him and we just looked at the street and the buildings for a while.

"Adam, let's go down the street a ways. I think you need to see a barber for a haircut and a shave."

Adam shook his head. "Ain't got the money for that. Tell you the honest truth I ain't even got enough for a shot of whiskey."

"Don't worry about paying for the haircut, Zack and me will take care of that. We'll even pay for a shot of whiskey later on."

Adam smiled and that gap in his teeth was

plain as anything. It added nothing to Adam's looks, but, in truth, there wasn't much that could in his case.

"That's right good of you boys. Only why are you doing this? You hardly know me."

"It's because we like you, Adam. We want to do something good for you. Can you understand that?"

Adam chewed that over for a while then said, "Sure. Let's go find that barber."

I helped Adam to his feet and the two of us took our time heading down the boardwalk. I glanced around now and then but I didn't see the Weezle boys anywhere in town. But I knew they were out there. Something in the back of my neck told me that. I only hoped that they wouldn't spoil Zack and my plan for the makeover of Adam Bellows. After all, we were only doing it for their loving mother.

It did not take very much coaxing on my part for the barber to allow us the use of his shop since there wasn't a single customer in the place when Adam and I got there. He was especially gracious when I offered to pay him a good sum for a shave and haircut and a place to change clothing.

Before he went to work on Adam, he put a sign in the window that the shop was closed.

Then Adam took the chair and fell asleep while the barber did a slow, but professional work on him.

As the barber was completing the shave, Zack rapped on the door and I let him in. He was carrying some store-boughts in his arms and he was certain they were Adam's exact size—or close to it.

Waking Adam, we had him strip down to his long johns and began dressing him in his new duds. When we finished and Adam stood before us the barber said, "A new man. Not the same one you brought into my shop."

It was eye-popping to see how much Adam had changed with just a haircut and a shave. He looked younger and cleaner and could pass easily for a man of some substance.

"Adam, you really look good," Zack said. "I mean that truly."

Adam glanced in the mirror. "Never thought I'd end up looking like such a dude. But I thank both of you. Some day I'll repay you for all your kindness. I really mean that."

I was almost tempted when Adam uttered those heart-touching words to drop the whole thing. Let Ma Weezle get angry, let her tell her boys to do what they did best. Then I re-membered the greedy, kill-crazy look in her three boys' eyes and I wasn't ready to meet my maker. Besides, things might just work out all to the good. I settled for not meeting my maker feeling that it would be easy for things to turn out all to the good.

As we stepped out of the barber shop there, standing in front of the hitch rail, were Lem, Bert and Handy. Our horses plus one more were tethered to the rail.

"You got what you come for?" Lem asked.

"Don't look like much to me," were Bert's words.

Handy was at least a little better-hearted. "Let Ma reckon on that. Let's saddle up and git for home."

The three Weezles mounted their horses and Zack, Adam, and me walked to the hitch rail.

"Where we goin'?" Adam asked in a soft whisper.

"Do not worry," Zack said. "We're with you and we'll take care of you."

"But they don't look very pleasant to me."

"It will be all right, Adam," I said, but my heart really was not in it. Looking at the brothers Weezle, I was suddenly reminded of how rough they were and how much rougher their mother was. I thought about telling Adam to ride away and let Zack and me get whatever

the Weezles had in mind for those who dis-
obey them.

Then Bert broke my thinking. "Let's move.
Ma's a-waitin' back at the ranch."

So we rode.

The ride back to the Weezle ranch was the
longest in my entire life. Adam did not seem
to mind; as a matter of fact he seemed cheerful
and happy as could be. Zack kept glancing
over at me and then Adam. I wondered if Zack
felt the same way I did. Like leading a poor
lamb to a fate worse than death.

I kept looking back at Spitville as it grew
dimmer in the distance. There was still enough
daylight to see the little town clearly. It wasn't
a place I would want to settle down in. Too
close to the Weezle family. They sure had
made a bad impression on the townsfolk at
Spitville. I wondered how long a town like that
could last.

These were my thoughts as each clop of the
horses' hooves brought us nearer to what dire
fate awaited us at the hands of Ma Weezle.

Lem, Bert, and Handy hadn't said a word to
any of us since we left Spitville. Yet every
once in a while I saw them steal a sneaky look
at the three of us. When they did so a sickening, evil smile crept across their dirt-splatter

faces. It sent chills up and down my spine, I had to admit. And Zack and me without any weapons to defend ourselves.

When we got to the ranch we slipped off our horses and Handy tied them to a rickety, old hitch rail.

"Go on inside," Bert said, and Lem went ahead of us to open the door.

"What's going on?" Adam asked. "Is this where I meet my lady friend?"

"Just go along with us, Adam," I said. "Trust us, please."

"So far you've been all right with me," Adam said.

I went in first with Adam following and Zack next trailed by Lem.

The inside of the ranch was still a wonder to me. Everything was neat, clean, and polished to a bright, clear shine.

"Nice home," Adam said.

"Quiet," Lem's voice crawled from behind us.

Out of a door off from the piano stepped Ma Weezle. She looked more wraithlike than ever. A curtain was drawn slightly and Ma stood in front of it. To put it kindly, it did little to bring out any feminine beauty in the woman.

"Who's that?" Bert asked.

"Quiet," Lem once again spoke. Lem was a man of very few words.

"So this is my suitor," Ma said as she walked toward us much like an overgrown spider about to feed on us poor, woeful flies.

"Yes, ma'am," Zack said none too convincingly.

"Well, take a seat, all of you," Ma said commandingly. "All except you, Lem. Stand guard."

"Yes, Ma," Lem said, and stood in the doorway, his arms folded sturdily across his chest.

In the meantime Zack, Adam, and me all sat down on a couch. Adam in the middle. Like before when Zack and me was in the house, Ma eased herself into a chair opposite us.

It was so quiet in that room I swear you could hear our hearts pounding. And why shouldn't they be? After all, this might be our last day here on this wonderful, golden earth. I thought about Cristobel and hoped that she would find happiness in Denver. I thought about the trail boss Wes Boone and wondered if he had found a cook yet for all those drovers. I wished that maybe Zack and me had never left the remuda for life in the circus. But if we hadn't we'd never met the wonderful folks there and I'd never have gotten a chance to be a trapeze actor. Wonder who Gunther got to replace me. It all seemed now like it had happened to another person.

"What's yer name?" Ma's voice jarred the quiet of the room.

"You speaking to me?" Adam said in a tone that made me swallow.

"I'm lookin' at you," Ma said.

"Then it's Adam Bellows."

Ma chewed on that for a spell, working her crooked mouth into an even meaner turn.

"Adam Bellows, huh! Sounds like a heifer calling to her mate." Ma Weezle laughed. The only thing worse than hearing Ma Weezle speak was hearing her laugh.

Lem, who had always done what his mother told him, laughed too. It was almost as earsplitting as his mother's. "Really good, Ma. Really good."

Ma turned an evil eye on her oldest and said, "Shut up, Lem."

Lem shut up. He always done what his mother told him to do.

"You ain't too much to look at, are you, Adam Bellows?" Ma said.

Adam didn't reply. He just sniffed as though he was smelling something offensive.

"Come to think of it, you two boys are a right disappointment to me." Ma's evil eye burned into my and Zack's flesh.

"Git 'em out out of here, Lem," Ma said as she settled back in her chair.

"What'll I do with them, Ma?" Lem asked.

"They're trespassin' on Weezle land, ain't they? Well, do what we always do to trespassers."

It was a horrible moment in my life. I wasn't about to give up without a fight. Even though Lem still carried his shotgun I would rather go down fighting than have folks say I was a coward.

Just as I was about to make a leap for Lem, something happened that was some kind of a miracle. Adam began to whistle, whistle through the gap between his two front teeth. It was the sweetest, purest kind of music I do believe I have ever heard in all my life. The sound filled the room and everyone in it seemed to be caught up in a kind of spell.

When Adam paused for breath Ma Weezle slumped in her chair and said, "Oh, you darlin' man, don't stop. That was 'My Dorie's Gone A-Wanderin'. It was Orville's and my favorite song."

So Adam, who enjoyed whistling, continued

the song and there were tears in Ma Weezle's eyes when he finished.

"You dear, dear man. Have you eaten anything today?"

"Not since last night," Adam said, leaning back against the cushions on the couch.

"You must be starvin'. You come with me to the kitchen and I'll fix you the grandest meal of steak and taters you've ever eaten."

"Sounds fine to me," Adam said, getting to his feet.

Ma came over and put a gentle arm around his shoulders. "And afterward I have some special strawberry pie. Then maybe you'll whistle me another one of them songs."

"My pleasure," Adam said as the two of them started for the kitchen.

I cleared my throat, loud and full of vigor. "Mrs. Weezle, what about Zack and me? Are we free to go?"

Ma weezle tossed a smile that would have melted the North Pole. "Lem, you and the boys make sure these two have all the makings they need for while they are on their trail. My thanks to the both of you."

Before the two of them went into the kitchen Ma said, "Of course you both are welcome to come to the wedding."

I said nothing because by the time Ma Weezle and Adam Bellows got around to wedding bells I hoped Zack and me would be hundreds of miles away.

Later on Zack and me rode along and I said, "Sure hope Adam and Ma Weezle will be happy."

"I just hope Adam never loses one of those front teeth."

We rode away.

Out there, somewhere, I always thought to myself, I'd meet up with Monk Hastings. I didn't forget Uncle Looty; I couldn't forget.

Chapter Six

Two days later we had left the Weezle family, Adam Bellows, and Spitville far behind but not out of our thoughts.

At night around the campfire after supping on the fixin's that the Weezle brothers had provided, we spoke of our last adventure.

"What if we hadn't been rounded up by the sheriff and thrown in jail?" I said to Zack. "We never would have met up with Adam Bellows."

"And we might still be in Spitville. With our names carved on tombstones."

"It was more than just fate, Zack. We were being taken care of. If you know what I mean."

"Sure do. You know, I don't even miss the

money we spent on making Adam look proper."

I laughed. "We really didn't need to. All it took was Ma Weezle hearing his whistle. He could have looked like the last wrangler in Abilene and Ma wouldn't have cared."

"Never would have figured it could end that way. No accounting for the way to a person's heart. At least we got enough vittles and stuff to last us a long, long time."

We stirred up the fire because it turns chilly at night out here on the open range. Above us the sky was stretched as tight as a dried up cattle carcass. The stars blinked at us like so many pinheads and somewhere out there a coyote wailed at the silver moon. I was content. After what had happened at the Weezle ranch I just needed a little peace and quiet.

"You ever wonder if Gunther will make a go of the circus?" Zack asked in a sleepy voice.

"Nope. That man is the last person I ever think about. But I gotta 'fess up that sometimes I do miss the music and the crowds and the noise of the circus."

"I miss the elephants," were Zack's last words before both of us called it a day and went to sleep.

It was the last night I dreamed about Ma Weezle and Lem, Bert and Handy and, of course, Adam Bellows and his whistling teeth. I could even hear that song he whistled. But it faded away that night and I never thought of it again.

A few days later Zack and me took our horses in to a blacksmith to have him check on their hoofs. While we waited we roamed about the town which was not any different from any of the others we had passed through.

There were several saloons, as usual, a mercantile store, a barber shop, and a few other businesses, not to mention the sheriff's office and the city jail.

Zack went into one of the saloons while I walked over to the mercantile store to browse around. While I was in there I bought a bottle of soda pop and then went outside to sit on the wooden bench to watch the townsfolk pass by.

About an hour or so later Zack met me at the blacksmith's and we paid for our horses and rode out of town. There was a fierce wind blowing and the air was filled with grit and sand and we decided to hunker down near some shade trees and wait out the bad weather.

The wind howled like a lost ghost but we were protected by the trees. Zack and me braced our backs against a tree for something steady to hold on to.

As the wind began to fade I thought I still heard the howling or soft wailing noise.

"Do you hear that?" I said to Zack, who had been listening too.

"It's not the wind, that's for sure. More like a moaning sound."

I got to my feet to look around. Maybe it was some animal that had been hurt and was crying out in pain. Zack and me both cared about animals ever since we had worked with them in the circus.

Putting one hand over my eyes to help keep the grit out, I made my way between the trunks of the trees. It wasn't easy and every once in a while a new burst of wind made me stop and cover my face with my hands.

It was while one of those gusts stung my face that I stumbled upon the body. Not a dead-and-gone body, but a sick and pain-ridden body. The man was moaning and that had been the sound Zack and me had been hearing.

I knelt down to get a better look at the poor old feller. He was thin as a weed with long, stringy gray hair. When he opened his eyes they looked like he wasn't long for this world.

"You're sick, old man," I said. "Can you tell me what ails you?"

He shook his head and even that seemed to hurt his whole body. "Started last week. Been getting worse every day. Go away. Leave me be."

I told him I couldn't do that. I called out for Zack and when he got here the two of us carried the poor creature back to where we had been hiding from the sand storm.

"What's your name, old man?" Zack asked. "What'll we call you?"

"What difference does that make. You'll just rob me and leave me here to die."

"No we won't," I said. "We're here to help you. I'm Horace and this here's my good friend Zack."

The old man closed his eyes and after a few minutes opened them again. He looked first at me and then at Zack.

"Guess you two can be trusted. I'm Pete. Pete Irish. Only I ain't Irish. Don't know where my family got that name."

I felt Pete's forehead. He was on fire and now and then he would shake like he was chilled. I got my blanket from my horse and wrapped Pete in it. That seemed to help the poor, sick man out but he still had a high fever.

We stayed with Pete until the storm blew over then we built a fire and I cooked some broth and spoon-fed Pete, who could barely swallow even that small portion of food.

During the night Zack and I took turns watching over Pete. We put damp kerchiefs across his forehead and that seemed to help the sick man out. When I was with Pete he spoke about how he had lost his mule who had wandered away when the storm set in.

"Bonnie is out there somewhere. Sure wish you or Zack could find her for me."

"We'll look for her tomorrow, Pete," I said. "Bonnie might even come back on her own."

"Never know about mules," Pete said before he drifted away for an hour or so.

Pete lingered on for a few days. Each hour he seemed to get weaker and weaker.

Bonnie wandered in one afternoon. The storm by that time was just something bothersome that had passed by.

The mule came close to where Pete lay and wouldn't move from where she stood. Zack had gone into town and brought some oats for our horses and we fed Bonnie along with them.

The night of Bonnie's return Pete sat up and said to me, "Git the packet that's strapped to Bonnie's back. Bring it to me."

I walked over to Bonnie, found the packet, and brought it back to Pete.

"Sit down. Close to me. You too, Zack. I ain't got much longer. It's the truth and you both know it. You two have been good to me. I want to repay you."

"You don't have to do that, Pete," I said, giving Zack a wink. What could this old, grizzled man have that he could share with us? Besides, we didn't expect any payment. We did what we did for Pete because we liked him and he needed help.

Pete shook his head. "I know I don't. But I want to and I will, dang it."

Pete untied the piece of rawhide that bound the folded piece of paper. Slowly he opened the paper and spread it out across his lap. It was a map of some sort.

"A few months ago, when I was a healthy man, I got in a poker game with this feller in Bisbee. He was runnin' short of money and I was runnin' high and wide, couldn't lose. It got down to his putting up this map against my stack of chips. He lost. I won. This here's that map."

Zack and me looked at the map. It didn't mean anything to me but Zack could read maps, something he picked up in his travels.

"That's El Diabo range, ain't it?" Zack said to Pete.

"Right as rain. And in that range there's a trunk full of gold. Gold stolen from a stage-coach hold-up years ago. The robbers buried it and drew a map so's they could find it later. Only one by one they ended up in Boot Hill. The map somehow got into this man's hands. He was playing for a stake to get supplies so's he could find that trunk."

I wasn't sure I believed Pete. He must be still suffering from whatever ailed him.

"I want you two to have this. I ain't got no kin. It's the least I can do for you helping me."

"We can't take this, Pete," I said. "You'll be up in no time and you can find that trunk of gold. You and Bonnie."

Pete growled. "I know what's happening to me. So here, Horace. This here map is yours and Zack's with my blessings."

It didn't do any good jawing with Pete. He was determined to give that map to me and Zack. To please him I took the map, aiming to give it back once he got back on his boots again.

Only Pete never did. We buried him a day later out here in the open plains, just as he wanted us to. Bonnie stood by his grave and wouldn't budge no matter what kind of coaxing came from Zack or me.

After we'd buried Pete, Zack asked to see the map Pete had given me.

"What good is it?" I said, reaching into my back pocket and having it over to Zack. "There's no gold buried in those mountains."

Zack unfolded the map and studied it. Studied it real close. After a while he said, "I got a hunch it's the real thing. And it's not too far from here. That's why Pete was in these parts before he took sick."

I still was not convinced.

"It's just a big hoax. How come nobody's found it until now?"

"Maybe because they didn't have the map. It shows right here where it's buried. Plain as anything."

As the day wore on and Zack wore me out, I was beginning to believe that it just might, just might be true.

"That's the way I want to hear you talk. For a while there I thought you might be losing your spirit of adventure."

So we decided to go treasure-hunting. Zack and me had tried many things—cooking, circusing, matchmaking to name a few, and now this. The more I thought about it, the more it got to me. After all, what was to keep Zack and me from doing it? We had no wives or children or even a share of land. It would be fun if nothing else.

"We'll need a few things from town," Zack said.

"Like what?"

"Picks or shovels. Something to dig up the treasure once we find it."

"I'll ride along. Might be something I will think of."

Bonnie hadn't strayed from Pete's grave and I had a feeling she would be there for the rest of her life. I hated to go off and leave her in case somebody came by and filched her. I left her a goodly supply of fodder then hurried to catch up with Zack who had gone on ahead.

By the time I rode alongside Zack we were nearly on the outskirts of the little town. The mercantile store was on a corner and we tethered our horses then went inside.

There were a few people inside, a man and his wife, two women looking at bolts of cloth, and two drovers who were just idling by the pickle barrel. One of them wore a black hat and had a flashy belt buckle around his waist. The other was a redhead with a week's growth of beard.

The owner came over and asked us what we wanted.

"A couple of good hardy spades for digging," Zack said.

"I think I have just what you are looking for," the owner said, and led us over to where he kept spades and shovels and rakes and other tools like that. "Will these do?" the owner asked, taking down two brand-new spades.

Zack held one in his hand and then pretended to be digging.

The owner laughed and said, "Practicing digging for gold are you?"

Zack laughed right back. "Might be. Might be at that."

We paid for the spades, bought some shells for our weapons, then left.

We rode through town for a spell to kill some time then headed back to our camp.

"I want to check on our supplies," I said. "I think we'll have enough to get by. How long do you reckon it will take us to get to El Diablo?"

"A couple of days' ride. Then we'll have to find a trail that goes to where the gold is. Probably have to even foot it part of the way."

That wouldn't bother me. I was used to walking back in Weed Patch, sometimes a couple of miles just to see if there was any mail for my aunt and uncle. But I never hiked in the mountains so it might be a whole lot different from flatland walking.

As we rode to our camp I kept getting this strange feeling like the short hairs on my neck were tickling me. Like maybe we were being followed. But when I glanced behind us all I could see was the worn, dusty trail. Just my imagination, I thought. Been out here in the wide, open country too long. Get to seeing things that aren't there and hearing noises you can't explain.

We decided to spend one last night at our camp and then get an early start in the morning. Bonnie was still standing guard over Pete and there would be no need for us to try to get her to leave with us in the morning.

Zack and I went gathering firewood and by the time we got back it was getting on to dusk. Away in the west I saw the El Diablo mountains, the range Zack had pointed out to me before. In the slowly dimming daylight the range looked craggy and mean, living up to its name.

We sat around the campfire eating our supper and Zack kept jawing about what we would find when we got to the place where the trunk of gold was buried.

"Just think, Horace, we'll be millionaires. We can buy anything we want. We can live anywhere we want and no longer will we have to work. Or work for any boss. Can't think of any better way to spend all that gold."

It sounded good but I wasn't all that loco about not working anymore. Uncle Looty had told me time after time that working was good for your hands and your peace of mind. I still think he was right and being all that rich wasn't what I wanted in life.

"You're awful quiet tonight," Zack said. "Anything itching your mind?"

I shook my head. "Just tired, I guess. Think I'll turn in. Want to be ready for tomorrow. Should be a big day."

"The biggest! One of the biggest."

The fire was burning low and I put a few more hunks of wood on it. I looked around to see if our horses were all right. Then I came back and lay down.

It was about an hour or so later that I awoke. The horses were acting nervous and snorting. Zack had heard it too and he was wide awake.

"What do you think it is?" Zack asked in a low voice.

"Maybe an animal. Lots of coyotes in these parts Just the same I'm going to have a look-see."

I reached for my gun that I kept near my saddle. Zack did the same. Then we got quietly up. Crouching so we wouldn't make a good target in case our visitor was a coyote, we circled around the camp until we came to the horses.

By the time we got there the horses were quiet and there wasn't a sign of an animal or anybody else.

"Guess they're gone by now," Zack said. "Probably just some animal smelling our food. The horses probably scared it away."

"I guess you're right," I said. "Let's get back to sleep."

Even though the horses and Bonnie had quieted down I still felt a little itchy and I put my weapon right beside me instead of under my saddle.

However, the rest of the night went by without any noise by the owl hoots and the faraway coyotes.

Morning came and I awoke to find a fire blazing and Zack making biscuits and frying bacon. But the best thing was the odor of coffee that never failed to bring me wide awake.

"Morning, Millionaire," Zack said as he poured himself a cup of coffee.

I got an empty cup and filled it. "You look eager and raring this morning."

"Time's a-wasting."

"Ease back, Zack. That gold, if there is any, has been there for years. A couple of more days won't make that big a deal."

"Suppose you're right. I just never had anything like this happen to me before. Had all kinds of dreams last night. Can't remember 'em this morning but I sure was one happy drover."

I couldn't help but laugh at Zack's jawing. I had had dreams last night too. And I couldn't remember them today. But they weren't all that uplifting. I drank my coffee, had some biscuits and bacon, then went to wash all the plates and cups in the stream not too far away from camp.

It wasn't until I had cleaned and scoured the plates with sand and started back to camp that I spied fresh footprints on the shore. Someone had been here during the night. There were two sets of bootprints and they led away, downstream. I decided not to say anything to Zack. Didn't want to spoil his high spirits.

We took our time packing our horses and

"Not too far away. Should be there tomorrow, you reckon?" I said.

Zack had come back from his sad thinking. He smiled and was his old self once more. "Early in the morning I'd reckon. Best we get to making tracks. The more we ride the closer we get to the fortune."

The sun was right over our heads as we put our Plainsman hats on and eased ourselves into our saddles. We rode until the sun had touched the ridges of the western mountains. The foothills were not too far away so we decided to ride just a little bit more so we could camp that night as close to El Diablo range as possible.

We found a group of outcroppings that made a perfect shelter and we gathered wood for a fire after we had taken care of our horses.

Supper was biscuits and beans that night and, for a treat, we opened a can of peaches. Sitting around the dying fire with our backs against the hard surface of the rocks, we were so tired the outcropping felt like down pillows.

"Hot peppers," Zack said. "Tomorrow is the big day. I can hardly wait. Don't reckon I'll get much shut-eye tonight."

"Don't bet on it," I said, then yawned. "We'll both sleep like babes tonight."

"Maybe. Maybe not," Zack said as he looked at something he had been glancing at ever since we left our first campsite.

"What's that you got in your hand?" I finally asked out of curiosity.

"Oh, this?" Zack held it out for me to see.

It was a compass. Just small enough to fit into Zack's shirt pocket.

"I wondered how you would know which way we should be going. A compass. You are full of surprises, Zack."

"Always ready. I picked this up in a pawn shop in Boise one weekend. Thought then it might come in handy. By cinders it did."

Zack put his compass away. I stared at the glowing embers and thought about what a lucky man I was. So much had happened to me since I left Weed Patch. And here I was with a good drover and maybe the two of us might come out with some really rich gold. That part was all right, it was just that I probably would have to think of someplace where I could put that kind of wealth to good use. I still had some money from the circus and just about all from the sale of Uncle Looty's farm. Enough for me. Yessiree. I was one lucky and happy farm boy. I turned on my side and for a moment I thought I saw a shadow move not too far from where we were camped. I squinted my eyes and stared in that direction for a spell. Then I reckoned it was just the moonlight playing tricks on me.

As I was about to close my eyes the sound of lightly falling rocks echoed in the dark.

I sat up. "Someone's out there," I whispered to Zack.

"Go back to sleep," Zack said in a tired voice. "It's just some rocks falling. Probably some squirrel or rodent started it."

I settled back down. Zack knew far more than I when it came to this kind of living. Maybe it was just a small landslide. Some tiny animals chasing another one. I was too jumpy. I felt to be sure my weapon was close by, just in case Zack might have been mistaken.

After a somewhat peaceful night Zack and me woke up to a chilly dawn. We got a small fire going and boiled some coffee. Neither one of us wanted to fix breakfast so we made do with the hot, steaming brew.

"It's going to be a rough climb from here," Zack said. "We'll have to leave the horses behind and go on foot."

I didn't mind. It would feel good to walk for a change after all the riding we'd been doing.

I glanced up at the high cliffs and the rugged outcroppings. Surprisingly I saw some pine trees that struggled out of the rocky soil.

"Ready?" Zack asked.

"Let's go."

Zack led the way, and that was surely fine with me. All of this was new to me. I breathed in the pure mountain air and willingly followed Zack up a brief trail that some boots in the long-ago past had hollowed out. The trail didn't last long. Soon we were hand-over-hand climbing the sharp, jagged rocks. It was slippery, rugged going over shale that cracked beneath our feet and toeholds. A few times I almost lost my grip and started to topple backward but I caught my balance and managed to stay fairly close behind Zack.

"Doin' all right back there?" he called out once or twice.

"Just keep on going. I'll stay with you."

"Not much farther to go before we reach a wide place. We can rest there and I'll check the map."

That was good news to me. Although I felt good about straining the muscles in my legs and arms a few minutes' rest would be right fine.

In no time we had come to the open flat

shelf of El Diablo. When we got there Zack and me dropped to our knees, then to our backs where we rested while gazing up at the hazy blue sky.

When we were well rested I sat up and said, "How much farther we got to climb, Zack?"

Zack eased himself into a sitting position and pulled out Pete's map. He studied it real carefully for a few minutes then said, " 'Bout another hour we should be where the gold is buried. Are you still with me?"

"You just lead the way, I'll be right behind you. This ain't so bad once you get the kinks out of your legs."

"Thought you'd like the climb. Nothing like it to wipe the cobwebs out of your brain."

"That's the truth. Something about this mountain air that is most agreeable."

We were back on our climb before too long and this time it didn't seem such a miserable task. An hour went fast and just as Zack had foretold we reached another plateau.

"This is where they hid it," Zack said. "All we got to do is dig it up. Easy as that."

Well, maybe it wasn't truthfully all that easy. The ground was solid-packed from all the rain and snow and small landslides. Zack did a noble job of locating the near-exact location of the trunk of gold. We got out our spades and and set to work.

The sun was directly overhead by this time and the digging was probably the hardest part of our quest for gold. We had gone down into the earth a few feet when I struck something solid with my spade. At first I thought I'd hit bedrock and I groaned with dismay.

"You've found it, Horace!" Zack cried out. "Eureka! You've found the trunk. That ain't no hardpan."

We jumped and yelled like a couple of Pi-utes doing a war dance. It was one of the most exciting moments in my life, next to the time I done my first swing on the trapeze in the circus.

Finally we ran out of breath and we both stood there gasping for air and grinning like two Halloween jack-o'-lanterns. When we had calmed down so we could think like rational, civilized men we set to work digging around the trunk, then carefully lifting it from its hiding place.

The trunk was that heavy and Zack and me were short of breath and tuckered out when we finally got it out of the ground.

"You found it," Zack said. "You get the honor of opening it."

I raised my spade and with a quick, well-aimed stroke shattered the lock. Carefully I lifted the lid on the trunk and there were all those sacks of gold, still in fairly good shape.

Out of nowhere a voice spoke. "Nice of you boys to go to all that trouble. We'll just take that off your hands, if you don't mind."

We spun around to face the muzzles of guns held by Black Hat and Red Beard, the two men from the mercantile store in town.

"Easy now," Black Hat said. "Put them spades down. I think my bullet is a lot faster than you can throw that spade."

"Who are you?" Zack asked. "How did you get here?"

Red Beard spoke this time. "Remember us from town? We heard you talkin' about diggin' for gold. We thought we'd see if you guys would get lucky. You were easy to track."

I hadn't been wrong when I had those feelings we were being followed. First at the campsite when I found those footprints. Last night it wasn't any animal on the mountain slope, it was these two. They were those dust devils I saw on the plains. I should have known we were being followed.

"Like I said, put them spades down, right now," Black Hat said. "Real easy now. Nobody will find you two up here. Not even when the buzzards start circling."

Zack and me slowly put down the spades. This wasn't the way things were supposed to work out. We had found the trunk after looking for it all this time. We had even dug the thing up.

Zack wasn't about to give the gold up that easily. "Look," he said. "There's plenty for all of us. We can share what's in the trunk."

"There will be more for just the two of us," Red Beard said with a smirk on his face. "Step back. I don't want to get any blood on the trunk."

Slowly Zack and I walked backward until we were a ways from the trunk. It seemed like me and Zack were always on the wrong end of pistols and shotguns. It didn't seem fair. Red Beard and Black Hat walked over to the trunk. They reached inside and each took a bag of gold. They still kept their weapons on us. I wondered how long Zack and me had on this great, good earth.

I was so nervous I thought my legs were beginning to tremble. Then I looked at Zack and I saw he was doing the same thing. Then I looked at the trunk, it was swaying back and forth and Black Hat and Red Beard were sway-ing with the trunk.

"What's happening?" Red Beard shouted, and his voice had a quiver to it.

"I don't know," said Black Hat. Then it came to all four of us.

"Earthquake!" I shouted.

At that moment the mountain began to groan and moan and the earth beneath Black Hat and Red Beard split open. They could have jumped to safety but they greedily hung onto the sacks of gold. The earth opened wider and wider and in a split-second swallowed both men, the trunk, and all the sacks of gold. Neither man had time to even cry out before the earth closed again, crushing them inside.

I fell to the quaking earth and Zack was down next to me. There was nothing to clutch or hang on to but small tufts of grass. I thought for a minute Zack and me were goners. I shut my eyes as tight as I could and waited for the ground to open up and swallow Zack and me. But it didn't.

It was all over so quickly and finally that I had a hard time believing what I had seen. The earth quit trembling and it was so still you could hear the wind whispering through the pine trees.

Finally I turned to Zack and, when I could speak, said, "I can't believe it. What do you think, Zack?"

Zack just shrugged as though nothing had happened. "Easy come, easy go," he said, and then kicked a spade furiously with his booted foot.

Chapter Seven

After the loss of the trunk of gold, Zack seemed to lose interest in adventuring. I found him at times gazing at the horizon, like he was seeing something that nobody else could see.

One day, while we were on the trail, he turned to me from his saddle and said, "Horace, this is as far as I go with you. I need to go home. Back to Montana. Can't explain it. It's something I have to do. Do you understand?"

Maybe I did, maybe I did not. All I knew was I was losing one real, true, and honest best friend. Then, instead of asking Zack to stay, I said, "I understand. Something you gotta do."

When you have a good friend you don't

stand in their way when they have to leave you. Even though they are gone, they will still be good friends.

Zack wasn't the kind of man who said, "So long." He didn't like those words. So, I awoke one morning to find he was gone. Zack, his horse, his belongings, all had vanished. It was almost as if he had never been there at all.

I fixed a lonesome breakfast that morning. The coffee didn't taste good, the biscuits were too hard, the bacon too greasy. Nothing seemed right. But I couldn't jaw about it since I was the only drover I could jaw to. So I got on my horse and rode away. Off to the west, to see what adventures lay ahead.

I roamed the west, stopping here and there, spending some time in one place and then another, seeing if I could find any clues that would lead me to Monk Hastings. I never truly forgot Zack but with time I met new folks, made a lot of friends. For some reason folks take to me. Maybe it's because I deep-down really like folks.

One afternoon I was in New Mexico or Arizona, at the time I didn't know which when I crossed the mountain range. There, below, spreading out was a long, deep valley.

From the moment I saw Hardscrabble I knew it was the end of my wanderin'. It was just like any other valley I had seen. Some were green, some were bigger, some had homes built fine and to last. Hardscrabble Valley was none of these. Yet I knew this was where I would settle down.

Hardscrabble wasn't really its true, original name. I think a man told me it was once called Prosperous Valley. To some folks that name was far from the truth. Those were the ones who settled for a spell then skedaddled when times got trying or tough.

Then there was the others. Folks like Lemuel Lukas and his wife and ten children. They loved Hardscrabble, said it was God's special gift. Anyway, it beat the cold winters they had suffered through back in the Dakotas. And there was Graff Bigsley, a widower and his five boys. They didn't seem to mind driving the water wagon clear up to the mountain and the stream to haul water back for their ranch. Hardscrabble, it seemed, had no water to speak of.

But I am way ahead of my life story. When I sat on my horse gazing down at the valley I realized what I had been missing. A place of my own. I had never owned any property in my entire life. Maybe I would be lucky and find a ranch or a small plot of land I could buy.

I snapped the reins and trotted down the mountainside. The trail was well-worn and easy on my horse. When I reached the foot of the mountain I was at one end of Hardscrabble.

Not really in any big hurry, I rode down a twisting road that was actually a trail that horses and wagons had widened over the years. Ahead of me I saw a house and there was movement in front of it. Signs of life.

I prodded my horse to hurry that I might ask whoever lived in the house just where I was and what was the name of the valley. As I neared the house I saw a man leading a team of horses to a corral. When he saw me he shooed the animals inside and closed the corral fence.

Approaching the man I touched the brim of my Plainsman and greeted him. "Good day to you. Name's Horace Featherbone."

The man nodded. "I'm Sam Spooner."

I said, "I'm a stranger here, could you tell me exactly where I am?"

The man nodded again. "Hardscrabble Valley, they call it. Look around, you can see why."

I looked around but what I saw was by no means a meager stretch of land. True, there was no grass, no trees, no flowers, but that didn't mean it wasn't impressive. I said as much to Sam Spooner.

"You can have it. All of it. I'd sell this place real cheap if someone made me an offer."

I made him an offer. Half of the money I got from the sale of Uncle Looty's Missouri farm. Of course it was all in fun.

"Sold," Sam Spooner said. "The ranch house, the land, the furniture, what there is of it. I'll sign it over to you right here and now."

This was going too fast for me. I said as much to Sam Spooner. "You can't truly be going to let this place go for that much."

"Sure can. It's mine to do with as I please. Now that my wife up and left me for a bunkum salesman that was passing through, I'm going back to Virginny."

I was beginning to believe what Sam Spooner was saying. If it was the truth then my longing for a home of my own was soon to be over and done with.

"But what about your children?"

"Got none."

"How you aimin' to go back to Virginia?"

"I'll ride all the way. Won't be any misery for me."

There wasn't anything else for me to ask. I slipped down from my horse and reached for the money from the sale of Uncle Looty's farm. Sam had gone inside the house and in a few minutes returned with some papers. He signed over the land to me and I gave him the money he had asked for.

Without another word, Sam got on his horse and with a wave of his hand galloped away.

I watched Sam until he was just a galloping speck of dust on the horizon. Then I read the piece of paper he had signed over to me. When I finished I realized I indeed was now the new, legal owner.

Taking a stroll around the place I saw there was a corral in need of repair, a team of horses, a buckboard, a small outbuilding, and feed for the horses for many months.

I then went inside the adobe house and looked around. There was a main room, a bedroom, and a kitchen, with pots and pans and plates and knives and forks. Mrs. Spooner had not kept a very neat house, but there were brooms and mops and cleaning powders. The windows let in sunlight that took away part of the gloom. The main room had good, sturdy furniture—something I felt Sam Spooner had made himself. There was a closet off of the bedroom and I found sheets and blankets and towels and washcloths.

All in all I had gotten the better part of the bargain with Sam Spooner.

Finished looking at the house, I went outside and over to the outbuilding where the hay was stacked and here I found pitchforks and tools I could use like saws and hammers and nails and things.

Back in the house I found that Mrs. Spooner had canned some peaches and pears and even some jars of meat. At least I wouldn't starve. Outside the kitchen was a huge barrel that was half filled with water. I would have to find out how to refill it from a neighbor.

But the first thing I had to do was look at the land I had bought and paid for. The papers had said there were markers, cairns they called them, piles of rocks to show me the property lines.

I got back in the saddle and rode until I found the first cairn—with a red kerchief on a stick stuck in it. The second one should be somewhere beyond this one. So I rode on.

I was happy and thinking about my good fortune at having my very own home when I didn't notice the girl until she was not too far away.

"You're new here," she said in a voice that was gentle as a newborn lamb but strong as a thundercloud.

"I am. I just bought Sam Spooner's ranch. Name's Horace Featherbone."

She smiled and the sun hid behind a cloud because it was so jealous.

"I'm Shasta Collins. Welcome to Hardscrabble Valley."

"Going to like it here. It's the first piece of land I've ever owned."

"Sam decided to go back to Virginia, did he."

"That's right. He's on his way right now."

"Too bad about his wife. Just didn't like ranch living. Hope your wife does."

I shook my head. "No wife. Not married."

Shasta smiled even wider. "Same here. Not married that is. I won't get married until I find the right man. The one who will put up with me and my writing."

The first time I have ever met a writer. Shasta got more and more interesting.

"Published?" I asked. "I would like to read some of your writing."

"Not published yet. But someday I will be."

I nodded. "I'm sure you will."

Shasta leaned back and looked over her shoulder. "Me and my father live back there. It's called the Dry Bar Ranch. Mostly because water is so scarce around these parts."

"Sure am getting aware of that. How do I get my water?"

"Take your buckboard and some barrels and go to the hills. There's a small lake there. That's what me and my father do."

I thanked Shasta and then she said, "Why don't you come over for supper tomorrow night? You might want to meet my father. Come over at six-thirty. Want to do that?"

I tried not to show too much enthusiasm but it didn't do any good. "I'll be there," I said, and Shasta reined her pinto and rode away.

I couldn't keep my eyes off of her as she rode away. Shasta was as beautiful as her name. And she was nice and friendly and rode her pinto well. Besides that she was bright enough to be a writer. Hardscrabble Valley was going to be good to me. I just knew it.

With a light heart I rode on to find the other cairns and see how much land I had bought. It was a lot, quite a lot. Sam Spooner did not realize what he had just about given away.

Only thing that I could see that was not very

favorable in the valley was the lack of water. It was a desert. Dry brush, hard, crackly sand, and not a tree in sight. At the moment I didn't care. If I got the land then I would find a way to grow things on it.

I headed back to the ranch, now and then glancing to the west where Shasta lived on the Dry Bar Ranch. She was on my mind all the rest of the day.

I cleaned and mopped the floors, dusted furniture, made the bed with clean sheets and a warm blanket. There was a sofa that was long enough for me to sleep on in the main room. But after all those nights sleeping on the ground with my saddle for a pillow the idea of my own bed and pillow was more to my liking.

As it turned dusk I went to the outbuilding and gathered some hay for the animals. My horse fit right in with the others and they seemed to welcome him as much as he was pleased to be in the corral.

I still had some vittles that I had brought in from my horse that I fixed for my supper. I found some kerosene lanterns that gave me plenty of light to see by.

Being tired from all the excitement of the day, I went to bed as soon as it was dark outside. The last thing I saw in my mind before I fell asleep was sweet Shasta's smiling face.

When morning came and I woke up I looked around nervously. Then, slowly, it came back to me that I was in my very own bed in my very own house. And I could sleep as long as I wanted to. Only I did not want to linger. There was still work to do and I wanted to take another ride on my land.

I found some flapjack mix and had some of it along with some bacon and coffee for breakfast. Then I went outside to see what needed fixing. Behind the house and next to the corral I found a small garden that still had some vegetables growing in it. The soil couldn't have been too dry if the Spooners had managed to grow tomatoes and beans and turnips. There was still some slightly wilted lettuce that I quickly cut and put in a pan of water inside the house.

Once again I went outside and began the work of repairing the corral. There was a pile of cut lumber behind the outbuilding that came in handy when I went to repair the corral fence.

It hadn't gotten too hot until around noon when I quit for something to eat and drink. As

I sat in the cool adobe ranch house I thought about seeing Shasta tonight and having a good-tasting meal for a change. I thought, too, about her father and hoped we would get along. I wasn't too worried since most people I met seemed to take to me.

After I'd eaten I went outside just as a lone rider came riding in. He was a big man with wide shoulders and a likeable face that displayed a lot of teeth when he smiled.

"Afternoon," the stranger said. "Graff Bigsley's the name. Saw Sam yesterday as he was heading out for Virginny. Said he sold out, so I thought I'd drop by and give my greetings."

I told Graff my name and offered him a cool drink of water. He gladly accepted.

We sat in the kitchen around the big mahogany table and Graff told me all about his family: five sons, no daughters. Wife had passed on two years ago but they were doing just fine.

"Was wondering how folks here in the valley make a living," I asked.

Graff told me that he and most of them had cattle that they let graze in the foothills. "Not enough water here for anything much to grow. If we had water in the valley it would make a whole lot of difference."

Then Graff spoke of the mining that went on in the mountains.

"What kind of mining?"

"Don't rightly know. Raven Collins keeps a tight hand on it. Nobody gets up there to see his operation. Nobody."

"Raven Collins? Is that Shasta's father? He owns a mine?"

Graff nodded. "Sweet girl Shasta, nothing like her old man. He's got a reputation in the valley and it ain't a good one."

Hearing those words was not too cheering for me since I was going to meet Raven Collins this evening.

Graff left shortly after we had finished our drinks. "Any problems, any trouble, you just call on me and the boys. Be glad to help out."

I echoed the same thing to Graff and he left. I knew I had made a friend in the valley.

Back to work I went and stayed with it until I realized I should wash up and get over to Shasta Collins's house.

I put on a fresh shirt, one I had found in the bedroom closet, one belonging to Sam Spooner. I polished up my boots and rode away to the west.

The Dry Bar Ranch wasn't hard to spot since the land was so flat and you could see for miles. When I rode up Shasta was on the porch, leaning against a support waiting for me.

"I'm so glad you could make it, Horace," Shasta said. "Take care of Mr. Featherbone's horse, Frank."

Frank was a tall, sullen man who had a slash for a mouth and hard, cruel eyes that had seen more than a lot of life. He took the reins of my horse and tethered them to the hitchrail.

"Please come in, Horace," Shasta said, and I followed her inside the house. It was comfortable and looked as if a lot of money had gone into the decorating of the living room.

"Would you care for some cider?" Shasta asked when I stopped gawking around. I thanked her. She went to a punch bowl and came back with two cut-glasses filled with the cider.

"How are things at your new home?"

"Couldn't be better. Got it all spruced up and I even had a visitor already."

Shasta was curious. "Who was that?"

"Graff Bigsley stopped by. We had a good talk. Seemed to be a right nice neighbor."

"Graff Bigsley is a no-account," came a loud voice from across the room and I almost spilled my cider as I turned to see a mountain of a man standing at the entrance to the dining room. "Don't listen to anything that lout has to say."

"Father, please." Shasta's voice for once was sharp and knife-like. "We have company. This is Horace Featherbone. He bought Sam Spooner's old place."

"Old is right, 'bout to come crashing down. That table in there set for us three?"

"Of course," Shasta said. "I've asked Horace to stay for supper."

"Just like your mother, always headstrong. Didn't consult with me about any supper. Well, never mind. I won't be having any tonight. Trouble at the mines," Raven started to leave and walked past me. "Good to meet you, Hector."

"Horace," I said.

Raven just snorted and walked out of the room slamming the door behind him. I could see Shasta was upset over the way her pap had acted.

"Got a real nice place here, Shasta," I said, trying to get her mind off her rude father.

Shasta smiled and was her old self once again.

We went into the dining room and the supper was just as I had imagined. As we were eating the pecan pie Shasta finally spoke of her father.

"Father can be so rude sometimes. Lately he seems to withdrawn, so secretive about things. We never were very close. Father wanted a boy and then I came along. Mother died a few years ago and I miss her. She and I were really close. Each day Father and I become more and more strangers to each other."

I felt sorry for Shasta but I didn't say so because I had a feeling she didn't want people to have that idea of her.

We went outside to the porch after supper and sat watching the moon and the stars come out. I had never felt this way about a woman before, even Loueena Barnloft. Shasta was special in every way.

Before I left she said, "Thanks for coming, Horace. I enjoy your company. I hope we see each other again. Soon,"

"You can count on it," I answered as I lifted myself into the saddle of my horse I had gotten from the hitchrail. "It was the best supper and the best evening I ever spent."

Having said that I rode away. All the way home I could think of nobody else but Shasta. I was sorry she and her father didn't get along.

Otherwise everything was just about as perfect as it can get at the Dry Bar Ranch.

I took my time riding home because I didn't want the night to be over yet. I had this loco notion that as long as I was in the saddle and riding, the night was still Shasta's and mine.

Finally I had to lead my horse onto the trail that wound its way to my ranch. When I got there I took care of the animal before shutting it inside the corral and locking the gate.

As I started for the house I thought I heard a noise from the outbuilding. I froze and waited but there was nothing. Probably the wind, I thought. It must have made a noise when it whistled through a loose board in the outbuilding. I thought tomorrow I would see to it. Right now I was happy and tired and ready for bed. Tomorrow would be another work day on the ranch.

I went inside, had a glass of water, and went to my bedroom. I undressed down to my underwear and crawled beneath the blanket. Thoughts of Shasta kept spinning around in my head. I just couldn't stop thinking about her.

I watched the pattern on the ceiling from the moonlight coming through the window. It was making me sleepy and I was about to shut my eyes when a shadow moved across the open window and then was gone. It wasn't the shadow of an animal but of a person. There was somebody walking around outside.

I got up quietly and slipped on my pants. I eased myself over to the window and peered out. Whoever it was had gone. I decided to go outside and make certain.

As I headed for the doorway I heard the faint sound of the the kitchen door open. I had forgotten to lock it when I went to bed. I looked around for something to defend myself with and grabbed a kerosene lantern that sat on the dresser. Slowly I moved through the house until I came to the kitchen. I stood in the doorway, kerosene lantern in hand.

Moving through the kitchen was a small, short person. He was touching everything he came in contact with like pots and pans and dishes.

By this time I had had enough.

"You there," I called out. "Don't move."

Surprisingly the person stood still as I lighted the lantern. To my surprise my intruder was a young boy. He was clad in ragged, dirty clothing and he looked like he hadn't had a bath in weeks.

"I won't move," the boy said. "Sorry, but I was hungry. I wanted something to eat."

The boy's honesty touched me. I put the lantern down and moved closer to him.

"What's your name, boy? How did you get here?"

The boy sniffed and wiped his nose on his dirty shirt sleeve. "Johnny is my name. Johnny Clover. I walked. Been walkin' for weeks and months."

"Where are your folks? Won't they miss you?"

"Ain't got none. After Ma died Pap started drinking and gambling. Lost everything, the house, the furniture. Everything. They found him in an alley one morning. When that happened I started out on my own. Just wanderin'."

I could understand Johnny. I'd lost everyone myself. "You're hungry, you said. Sit down, Johnny. I'll fix you some vittles."

As Johnny ate he told me stories of how he had roamed all over the west. Sometimes he slept in abandoned houses, sometimes in orchards. He just had to keep moving.

After he ate and I'd listened closely to him, I decided he could stay on. There was honesty in his words and he needed needed a place to stay.

"Go wash up," I told him. "You can sleep on the sofa."

While he was cleaning the filfth from his body I went to the closet and found a shirt and a pair of pants that were a little too long but would be better than what he had on.

The boy looked thankful and tired and I made a bed for him on the sofa.

"What's your name?" Johnny asked before he shut his eyes.

"Call me Horace," I said, and Johnny smiled and was gone to sleeping.

The next day Johnny helped me around the ranch and he was a good and willing worker. He was like the little brother I never had. The day following I had a visit from Graff Bigsley who told me there was going to be a barn raising today at Clem Lukas's ranch. I told him me and Johnny would follow him over.

When I told him about Johnny Clover he looked at the boy and said, "Them ain't too good a fit of clothes. One of my boys is Johnny's size. I'll have him bring some of his things over."

Johnny was accepted without questioning by the folks in the valley that day. He was a hard worker and Clem Lukas's wife took to him and said she could fix some of the Bigsley boys' shirts and pants so Johnny wouldn't look so bedraggled.

I was pleased when Shasta showed up with baskets of food she had fixed. I got the feeling that while Shasta was well liked her father wasn't welcome in any home in the valley.

When I was resting Shasta came over with some fried chicken and potato salad and lemonade. We ate together and I told her about Johnny, how he had wandered in and I had sort of took charge of him.

Shasta smiled. "That was nice of you. He's just a boy. I'm glad you are helping out today. Gives me a chance to see you again."

"Been writing?" I asked.

"Always," was her answer. "I just cannot stay away from it. Just something I am compelled to do."

"Keep at it. You'll be published some day."

Shasta nodded and said, "One of these days, like this Saturday, I'll fix us a picnic lunch and the three of us, you, me and Johnny can ride to the foothills for an outing. Would you like that?"

"More than anything," I said and I meant it.

Shasta had to leave then and go about giving out food with Clem's wife at her side.

Graff came by to sit for a spell. "Nice girl," he said, meaning Shasta. "Too bad her father doesn't take after her."

"Why does everybody put down Raven Collins?"

"He's a mean one. And he treats his help like they was clods of dirt and Shasta too. That and what he's up to on his mining claim."

I listened closely, maybe I would learn something that would help me figure out who Raven Collins really was.

"He's got something going on up there that ain't just right. Man, if he's honest, has no need for armed guards at his mine. Nobody can come within a hundred feet of the place without meeting the mean end of a rifle."

It didn't sound good for Raven Collins but before I could learn any more Graff said we'd better get busy, only got a little bit of work left on the barn.

I got so busy, along with Johnny and the rest, that Raven Collins and his mine just left my mind. When we got home Johnny and I washed up and sat on the porch for a spell but we were both too tired to linger and we went to bed.

The next day Graff came by with two of his sons and he asked to take Johnny into town with him. I thought it was a good idea. Before he left I slipped some money into Johnny's shirt pocket so he would feel like he wasn't poor relations.

When they had gone most of the work on the ranch was done and what little remained I needed Johnny to help out. So I saddled up and went for a ride.

I headed for the foothills and the mountains beyond. Mostly I wanted to find the small lake Shasta had mentioned for future use.

The day was warm and cloudless. I relished being back in the saddle once more. It reminded me of my days with Zack Hockenbrew and the good and bad times we had had together. I wondered if Zack was in Montana by now and if he had, like me, decided to settle down.

It didn't take me long to reach the foothills which were small mounds of earth and rock that were webbed with trails folks had made over the years.

I kept an eye out to see if I could spot the lake Shasta had talked about. I rode along, enjoying the scenery and being alone for a while. I thought about what my future was going to be here in Hardscrabble and what kind of a living I I would make. The money from the sale of Uncle Looty's farm would not last forever.

All these thoughts went through my head and I wasn't paying all that much attention to my surroundings. Suddenly there was a sharp crack from a rifle and a ping as the shell smashed into a rock.

I drew the reins to calm my horse and looked up at the top of a boulder. There stood Frank, the hired hand I had seen at the Dry Bar Ranch the night I had supped with Shasta.

"No trespassing," Frank called out. "Come any closer and you are buzzard fodder."

"I didn't see any signs," I said, getting really angry.

"They're there," Frank said. "This here's Raven Collins's mine. So turn around and head back the way you've come. Understand?"

I think Frank wouldn't have minded in the least squeezing the trigger on his rifle. At least he wasn't the Weezle brothers—there was just one of him.

I slowly eased my horse around and headed back down the trail I had been following. Once I turned my head to look back but Frank was nowhere to be seen. I didn't want to test him to see if he would mysteriously appear again.

All sorts of thoughts went through my mind as I trotted back down the trail to the valley. What was so important in the mine that Raven Collins had a guard posted? Graff had said there were several guards, they must have been farther up the mountain nearer the mine.

Surely in this valley which was made up of peaceful family-type folk there was no need for such secrecy. So far I hadn't met a scoundrel in the lot of them. I worried then about Shasta. Graff had said Raven treated his hired hands poorly and Shasta the same. If I ever heard of him doing any harm to her he would have to answer to me. Even if he was a mountain of a man he didn't frighten me one little bit. I wasn't exactly a frail, scared rabbit myself. I pretty much felt if it came to a showdown between the two of us, I wouldn't be the loser.

I rode back to the ranch disliking Shasta's father as much as I liked her.

Chapter Eight

Saturday morning came and Johnny and I had some chores to do before I took the buckboard over to pick up Shasta.

Johnny was so willing to work that it was a real pleasure to labor beside him. When it grew late in the morning we washed up and Johnny donned some of the clothing Mrs. Lukas had altered for him. He didn't look a lick like the ragamuffin who had snuck into my kitchen not too long ago. I think he was happy living on the ranch and he put a lot of sunshine into my life. Besides, he was a great help around the ranch, always eager to help, never complaining about anything I asked him to do. Nothing was too hard for him to do.

157

Together we hitched up the team and rode over to the Dry Bar ranch. As I had expected, Shasta was on the porch waiting for us. I helped her into the buckboard and Johnny stowed the food in the back and settled himself there too.

"Where we bound for?" I asked Shasta, who pointed to the foothills.

"Follow that trail. There's a nice shady place in the foothills. Perfect for a picnic."

"Sounds great to me. Huh, Johnny?"

Johnny was agreeble as always. Shasta smiled at him and said he looked elegant in his new duds.

It was a fine ride to the foothills. We saw not a single other buckboard or wagon or even a lone ride. When we got there, Shasta had been right, as always, there were shade trees and even patches of soft, green grass.

"The lake where we get our water is not too far away," Shasta said. "Just in case you need to drive up to fill your barrels."

The three of us walked around and I never felt such joy and happiness in my life.

When we got hungry I spread out a blanket Johnny brought from the buckboard and we sat down to roast beef sandwiches, pickles, and cole slaw that would melt in your mouth.

We ate until we were stuffed then we sat on the blanket barely making conversation until Johnny pointed at the mountain and said, "I was up there once. The mine, I mean. I got by the two guards and got to see the Chinese workers in their hollowed-out caves."

"Chinese?" I asked. "Are they working at that mine?"

Johnny nodded. "One of them spoke a little English. He told me he and the others had been shanghaied into working there. The owner of the mine had them shipped from China after they had been drugged."

I glanced over at Shasta when Johnny had said the owner of the mine had paid to have Chinese labor smuggled in. Shasta hadn't seemed angry or hurt, she just shook her head. "It doesn't surprise me. I knew that Father was up to something the way he wouldn't tell me how we managed to be so wealthy when nobody knew what he was mining up there."

"But the Chinese," I said. "Why didn't they try to run away? Why did they stay?"

Johnny reached inside his pants pocket and pulled out a tin container. It had a colorful design on it and Chinese lettering etched across the design.

"Opium," Johnny said. "These tins contained opium. They are all over the place, that's how I got one."

"But the guards? How did you get in?"

Johnny shrugged. "I'm small, nobody really notices me. Besides, I've learned a lot of ways to get into places without being seen."

"When was all this?" Shasta asked.

"Just before I came to Horace's place. Not too long ago."

"We'll have to do something about this," I said. "We can't allow your pap to go on with this kind of crime."

Shasta sighed. "I know. I heard him telling Frank something about another shipment coming in tomorrow night."

"At the ranch?" I asked. "I mean will they bring the laborers to the ranch?"

Shasta nodded. "That's how it was done before, I'm sure of that now. Father wouldn't let me leave the house the night another wagonload of Chinese came in. He is such a vile man." She looked at me and Johnny. "I'm sorry but that's the way I feel. He never loved me or my mother. He only loved money."

We didn't linger much longer at the picnic. There was work to be done. Right away.

I drove Shasta back to her ranch and then Johnny and me drove the buckboard over to

Graff Bigsley's ranch. We were quite lucky in finding that Graff was home; he and the boys usually were tending their cattle in the foothills.

"I have to talk to you, Graff," I said when he came out of the ranch house to the buckboard. "It's about Raven Collins and what he's been up to."

At the mention of Raven, Graff was all ears. He had never liked the man and he would be willing to listen to anything that would cause his downfall.

As quickly as I could, I told him all about the Chinese laborers and how Raven had illegally brought them into the valley.

"Sounds just like something Raven Collins would do," Graff said. "No wonder he kept the mine's operation so secret."

"We've got to put an end to this," I said.

"When and where?" Graff asked.

"Tomorrow night. Are you with me?"

"Me and my boys. You can count on us."

That was good news for me but bad news for Raven Collins.

"I'll contact the rest of the men in the valley," Graff said. "What about the workers at the mine?"

"After we take care of Raven and Frank,

we'll go up to the mine. I don't think we'll meet with any problems there."

"Sheriff Davis out to know about all this," Graff said. "He's in town. He's a good man and an honest one."

I nodded. "I'll take care of that. I'll make a run into town as soon as I leave here."

We talked for a few more minutes about what time we would all meet at the Dry Bar Ranch.

"After sundown," I said. "That's probably when Raven will bring the laborers in."

It was decided then. I knew I could depend on Graff. He was an honest man who only wanted the best for the valley.

Instead of heading for town me and Johnny drove over to see Shasta.

We were lucky once more. Raven and Frank were not around.

"Father's up at the mine," Shasta said. "Or so he told me. I think he's gone to pick up the laborers."

It was not easy for me to tell Shasta of my plan. I tried to speak as gently as I could to her. She was very sweet and she understood.

"You are doing the right thing, Horace," she said. "I am not angry or hurt by your decision."

I couldn't have felt better as I left the Dry Bar Ranch. Shasta had made what me and the other men intended on doing so much easier. I could have tossed my Plainsman hat into the air and kicked my heels in the air. But I had Johnny with me and I needed to be a good big brother to him.

"Where to now, the sheriff's office?" Johnny asked.

"Right. Sheriff Davis is who Graff said we should see."

We rode as quickly as we we could to town. By this time Johnny knew his way around from going there with Graff and his sons.

"At the end of the street," Johnny said. "That's the sheriff's office and the jail."

I drew reins and brought the team to a quick halt in front of the jail.

"You stay here with the team," I said to Johnny and, as usual, he was agreeable as ever. "Be back as soon as I can."

"Take your time," Johnny said as he tilted his hat forward like he had seen me do when the sun was in my eyes.

I walked over to the jail and opened the door and walked inside. There was only one drover inside and it had to be Sheriff Davis. He was a medium-sized man, with a ready smile and a mane of white hair—too young for the color but maybe it went with the job.

"Sheriff Davis?" I asked. "I'm Horace Featherbone."

Sheriff Davis got up from behind his desk and smiled as he reached for my offered hand.

"Please to meet you, Horace. Been hearing some good things about you from the town-folks."

I guess I turned red because my face felt like I'd been in the sun too long.

"That's good to hear, Sheriff. Graff Bigsley said some right nice things about you too."

"Graff and his boys are good, law-abiding citizens. What can I do for you, Horace? Mind if I call you that?"

"Suits me fine, Sheriff."

After that we both took seats and I felt like I'd known Sheriff Davis for years. I felt free to tell him of Raven Collins and his illegal operation and what me and the men intended on doing.

"That is, Sheriff, if we can get your all-right."

Sheriff Davis nodded. "I've been thinking about Raven Collins for months. He is a wily man and a dishonest one. I'll go along with you and your idea Horace, on one condition."

"Name it, Sheriff."

"That I deputize all you men. Make it all legal in the eyes of the law."

"No trouble, Sheriff. I know the other men would go along with that. We just want to see Raven Collins behind bars where he belongs."

"When did you say all this was going to happen?"

"Tomorrow night, after sundown. At the Dry Bar Ranch. Reckon we will catch Raven when he brings in a new bunch of laborers."

Sheriff Davis shook my hand again before I left feeling I had made another good friend in Hardscrabble.

Outside Johnny was still sitting on the buckboard seat with his hat pushed down to shield his eyes.

He almost jumped when I climbed onto the buckboard and plopped on the seat.

"All set?" he asked, pushing his hat back from his forehead. "Did the sheriff go along with your idea?"

"He's a good man. Wants to deputize all the men. Sort of make things all legal like."

"Great!" Johnny said. "I always wanted too be a deputy."

I was about to tell him he wouldn't be joining the rest of us but when I saw the anxious look in his eyes I figured Johnny Clover had been through more scrapes and adventures than most men twice his age.

We rode back to the ranch and, to keep our mind off of what lay ahead tomorrow, we got to work on the corral, hammering and pounding nails. Late in the afternoon Clem Lukas came by on his horse.

"Just got through jawing with Graff," he said, leaning forward on the pommel of his saddle. "You can count me in. Never cared much for Raven but I feel sorry for Shasta. She's a good woman and deserves better for a father."

I told Clem I agreed with him and offered him a drink of water. He shook his head. "Thanks anyway, Horace. I've got to be getting along home. Just wanted to tell you I go along with you and your idea. All the way."

"Sometimes, being new here in the valley, I think maybe I'm acting out of turn. Sort of like a newcomer who wants to take over. Believe me, Clem, I'm not that way."

"You don't have to make no apology. You're the best thing that's come along in this valley for a long time. You got us men into action. We jaw a lot about Raven but none of us done anything about it."

That did help. I felt maybe that I was helping out, in the best way I knew how.

"See you tomorrow night, Horace. Sundown you say. And at the Collins ranch."

"That's right, Clem. And if you got a weapon, bring it along. That goes for any of the other men in the valley."

"Got you," Clem said, and then he spurred his horse and galloped away.

"It's true, everybody's bringing a weapon?" Johnny said. "Me too?"

I wasn't sure about that. I was counting on the gun Uncle Looty gave me as a birthday present. But there was a rifle I found in the bedroom closet. Must have belonged to Sam before he left so suddenly and clean forgot it.

"Maybe you can carry the rifle. But I don't want you to have an itchy trigger finger."

"One thing about my pap. When he was sober he taught me how to fire a gun. Used to put empty tin cans on fenceposts so's I could use them for target practice. Got pretty good at it."

Knowing Johnny, I was certain he told the truth. I just didn't want to be worrying about him if trouble came and Raven decided to make a stand.

Night came and we ate, then stayed up later

than usual just jawing. When the moon rode high in the sky we both yawned and went to bed.

I was restless, even though I was tired, and it took me a long time to fall asleep. When I did, as I expected, I had crazy dreams and nightmares. So did Johnny. I heard him talking in his sleep when I woke during the night. I checked on him but he was all right except his blanket had been thrown to the floor. I picked it up and put it over him again. He did not wake up.

The next day we kept busy but the night that lay ahead of us was on our minds.

When it finally grew dark we saddled up our horses and rode off to Shasta's ranch. There was a full moon that made everything bright as daylight. It was both good and bad. Fortunately there was a stable at the Dry Bar Ranch so that all our horses could be hidden away until Raven and Frank and the laborers appeared.

After we got to the ranch Shasta met us and told us we were the first to arrive.

"It's still early," I said. "Maybe you ought to stay inside, Shasta. We don't know how your father and Frank are going to take this. There's bound to be trouble."

"If you think so. But I'm going to be watching from my window to see what's happening. It's the writer in me."

Shasta went inside and Johnny and me took our animals to the stable. After we had settled them down we went outside to wait for the rest of the men to arrive.

We didn't have long to wait. Graff Bigsley and his sons were the first to arrive.

"You're the first," I said as Graff came over to the stable. "We're putting our horses inside. Don't want Raven to get suspicious when he arrives."

"Is he bringing the Chinese?" Graff asked.

"I don't think so. It's just a guess but I think he and Frank will probably ride up first and then whoever is bringing the laborers will show up later."

Graff went inside and soon afterward the men from the valley appeared. There was plenty of room in the stable and Graff told one of his sons he was to take care of the animals inside. The boy complained a little but Johnny volunteered to help him and that brightened the boy's outlook.

When Sheriff Davis rode in he quickly deputized all of us and he said he felt better about the whole idea now.

We had all settled in the shadows when we saw two riders approaching from the west. They had to be Raven and Frank. They took their time riding in and when they got to the ranch they eased themselves off their horses.

"When is Tabor coming with those coolies?" I heard Frank ask.

"Any time now. He was waiting till sunset to bring the wagon across the open desert."

"We're doing all right, ain't we, Boss? Maybe we can even start selling these coolies to other miners."

"Maybe," Raven said, and then he glanced around. "What's keeping that Tabor? He should be here by now."

Frank looked out across the land then he said, "He's coming, Boss. Out there. See his wagon?"

Raven didn't answer but looked in the direction Frank had gestured to.

"Something ain't right," I heard Raven say.

"What's wrong?" Frank said.

"I don't know. I got an edgy feeling tonight. Something just ain't right."

I hoped Raven didn't look too closely into the shadows. The full moon had moved toward the west so that the eaves of the outbuildings and the stable offered us good coverage.

All was quiet until I heard the sound of hoofbeats and the creaking of wagon wheels. Slowly the covered wagon pulled in next to where all of us were hidden.

Tabor, the man with the reins, said, "Sorry, got held up back there. Had trouble with one of the wheels."

"You got a full load?" Raven asked as he walked over to the wagon.

"Every last one of them."

Sheriff Davis at that moment decided it was time to make our presence known.

"Hold it right there, Collins," He said as he stepped out from the shadows. One by one the men followed him. With lightning speed Raven leaped onto the wagon and yelled at Tabor, "Move it! Move it right now."

Tabor was quick to obey and he cracked the whip, setting the team to galloping.

Frank was left alone but he wasn't to be taken so easily. He lifted his rifle and aimed it at Sheriff Davis but there was an explosion next to me as Graff got off a round from his own rifle. Frank dropped his rifle as he slumped to the ground.

"Get our horses!" I yelled at Johnny who had opened the stable doors.

In an instant Sheriff Davis, myself, and

Clem were on our horses in quick pursuit of the covered wagon.

Sheriff Davis rode by my left side and Lemuel was at my right. The wagon had a head start but it didn't take us long to draw close to it. The dust from the wagon wheels made from the trail made it hard for us to see but I caught a glimpse of moonlight on the barrel of a rifle as Raven took aim and fired. There was a cry from Clem who clutched at his shoulder.

This sent the bile boiling in me. Clem was a decent drover with a wife and children. He wasn't killed by the bullet but wounded. I made a quick grab for my pistol and I don't recollect firing it but I saw Raven drop his rifle as he fell from the wagon.

With Raven gone the spirit had gone out of Tabor and he reined in the team of horses until they came to a slow, rolling stop.

By this time Sheriff Davis had reined his horse and gotten down to kneel beside the body of Raven. I eased my horse to a stop beside the two of them.

"How is he?"

"Gone. Good, clean shooting, Horace."

I did not think that was such a compliment. Never having killed a man before, it wasn't the most happy of feelings. Especially since that man happened to be the father of the woman I had come to believe someday might be my bride.

I rode then to the covered wagon. The man called Tabor still sat holding the reins. I went to the rear of the wagon and peered inside to see a whole passel of frightened, huddled Chinese workmen.

I did not know if they could understand me so I yelled at Tabor, "Can you talk to them in their language?"

"I learned it," he said.

"Tell them not to be afraid. We are friends and we won't hurt them."

Tabor said some words I reckoned were Chinese. He must have repeated what I had told him because a change came over them and they clapped their hands and kept nodding at me.

Sheriff Davis came over to me with the body of Raven Collins slung across the rear of his horse.

"I'll put him up front with the driver," Sheriff Davis said. "Be more humane than letting Shasta see him being toted on the back of my horse."

I had to agree with him.

"Head this wagon back to the ranch," I said

to Tabor. "And don't try to make another run for it."

"Don't worry," Tabor said. "I ain't no hero. Do you have to put that thing in the wagon with me?"

"Get going," I said.

The four of us, along with the laborers and the body of Raven Collins, headed back to the Dry Bar Ranch.

I rode over to check on Clem who was holding his wounded shoulder with one hand and letting the horse take its head.

"How are you, Clem?" I asked.

"Be okay. Went through my flesh. Didn't crack a bone or anything. Thanks for saving my life, Horace. Raven's next shot at me might not have been so far off."

I could not say anything. I felt bad that a good man like Clem had to be shot and I also felt bad that a bad man had been killed.

Chapter Nine

The only sounds that we heard on the way back to the ranch were the Chinese as they sang some songs in their native tongue. It was a very strange and sad evening for me.

We got back to the ranch and all the other men gathered around us and the covered wagon.

When Graff saw Raven's body he said, "Hate to say this but good riddance."

At that moment the crowd parted as Shasta came toward the wagon.

"Where is he?" she asked, and I got down from my horse and led her to the wagon. Even though he had treated her badly all her life

Shasta, to her fine credit, moaned a little and there were a few tears.

"Better bring him inside. Would one of you men go for the undertaker?"

"I'll do that, Miss Shasta," said one of the men.

"Would you come with me, Horace?" she asked, and I took her arm to steady her as we walked to the ranch house.

Sheriff Davis and Clem followed us and behind us two men carried the body of Raven Collins.

Inside Shasta asked them to take his body into his bedroom. When they had done that they quietly and sadly left.

"I have some coffee made," Shasta said. "Couldn't we all stand a cup?"

We all agreed and followed her to the kitchen. Shasta poured cups and gave them out. When she saw the blood on Clem's shirt she made him take it off while she dressed the wound. When she had finished he drank his coffee then said, "Thanks, Miss Shasta. I'd better hit for home. My wife will be that worried about me."

Then, before he left, he said, "Sorry for you about your pap, Miss Shasta. But if it hadn't been for Horace, Raven would have taken a second shot at me and hit the mark. Horace's good shooting saved me, Miss Shasta."

I wished Clem hadn't said that. It wasn't the way I would have broken the news to Shasta. Surprisingly she sat down and put a hand on my arm. "I don't hold any anger toward you, Horace. You did what needed to be done."

I cannot begin to express what a relief it was to me to hear those words from Shasta and then have her touch my arm the way she did. She could very well have blamed me and never wanted to see me again. What a gentle, wise spirit this woman had.

We all sat and drank coffee until the undertaker got there. He called for Shasta and she pleaded with me to come along with her, which I willingly did.

The undertaker made the arrangements with Shasta and said he would get back with her if there was to be a funeral. Shasta told him right out, there would be no service—only a few words spoken at his graveside. As far as Frank was concerned, he had perished when he had been shot, the undertaker said it would be Potter's Field for him.

It was dawn before any of us realized it. Some of the wives of the men had arrived with food and they prepared breakfast since Shasta had too much on her mind to worry about that now.

Sitting around the table eating, one of the wives said, "The men in the wagon, what do you suppose they like to eat?"

"Great Judy, I forgot all about them," Sheriff Davis said. "I'll get them out and ask that Tabor fellow what vittles they cotton to."

After Sheriff Davis had left Shasta said, "We have to do something about those poor, forlorn people. Maybe we can find work for them in the valley or outside of it. Or we can ship them back home if they prefer. The Collins ranch will pay for their passage, of course."

"There are still some up at the mine," Johnny said. "Some of us could go up and bring them down."

Graff spoke up. "Maybe they wouldn't mind working the mine if they got a decent wage."

"Would you take care of that, Graff?" Shasta asked. "I would be grateful to you."

"Good as done," Graff said, getting to his feet. "I'll take Johnny and some of the men with me. There are still a few guards up there."

Johnny looked at me for permission and I nodded. He and Graff quickly left the house.

The undertaker took Raven's body away

wrapped in oilcloth. Frank's body, done the same, rode beside his boss in the wagon.

Slowly the folks began to leave with the promises they would be back with tents for the Chinese workers. Some of the men offered to hire some of the workers, through Tabor of course, and their offers were accepted with polite nodds and bows.

When the tents arrived I helped put them up and when we finished Johnny and Graff arrived with the rest of the work force.

"There wasn't much of a fight," Johnny said. "When the guards saw us coming with our guns and rifles they ran away to the hills."

Me and Johnny stayed with Shasta to make sure all the workers got to sleep in their tents. Sheriff Davis took Tabor away to spend the night in jail but would bring him back in the morning to do his translating. It remained iffy what legal action would be taken against Tabor since he was so urgently needed to make the workers needs known.

It was dark when Johnny and me rode back to our ranch. Tired, weary but somewhat content, we washed up then went to bed.

That night there were mixed-up dreams and several times I awoke in a cold sweat. The idea of killing a man was not something I could just shrug off. It bothered me then and it does to this very day.

For me the bad times and the killing were not quite over. Johnny and me had ridden into town for some supplies when I, by some miracle, saw someone who bore a strong resemblance to Monk Hastings treading down the boardwalk.

I reined in my horse a ways ahead of him and met the mean, thieving layabout as he approached. "Monk Hastings, remember me?"

Monk stopped in his tracks, his face turning a shade whiter than new-fallen snow.

"In case you don't, then maybe my Uncle Looty and Aunt Millie will jog your memory."

From where I stood, real close to him now, I could see sweat-drops sting his forehead. "Don't reckon I do. Must be mistaken."

"Don't think so." I was patient. "You stole my uncle's savings and you set fire to his house. With him and my aunt tied up inside. And now you've got to answer for what you did."

I intended to walk Monk Hastings over to the sheriff's office at gunpoint. I wanted to see him hang after the world heard of his horrible crimes.

Monk reached quickly for his holster and

the six-shooter. But I was quicker and my weapons blasted two holes into his chest. Monk had a surprised look on his face as he crumpled to the boardwalk.

There was enough money left from Uncle Looty's savings to just bury Monk Hastings on Boot Hill. Nobody but the undertaker attended the burial. That day, I felt peace knowing that Uncle Looty and Aunt Millie's senseless deaths had been accounted for. I could truly move on now with my life instead of living like a nomad.

Over the next few days Johnny and me were at the Dry Bar Ranch more than we were at my spread.

Slowly we managed to find places, good places, for the Chinese workers and when the last one had left Shasta said to me, "I will be going to Ohio for a while. I have an aunt there who wants to see me. I just have to get away for a while, to think things over. Do you understand, Horace?"

I said I did yet in my heart I wished she would stay. I couldn't think of how the valley would be without her. Just knowing Shasta was only a brief ride away was such a comfort to me.

After she had gone I tried to keep busy. Johnny and me rode out to the land that was marked with cairns.

"Why don't we put some wooden posts in?" Johnny said. "Then we wouldn't have these piles of rocks."

Sounded good to me, so we went back to the ranch and loaded up some of the lumber Sam Spooner had left behind. We put the lumber in the buckboard and rode back to the range.

It was while we were working on the second cairn that it happened. Johnny was holding the post steady while I was in the buckboard with a sledgehammer pounding away when suddenly the post sank deeply with a thud and Johnny let go as it shot back to the surface. When it did so a fountain of water gushed forth.

"We done it!" Johnny cried, dancing around under a geyser of spraying water. "We done struck water."

I couldn't believe it and for a few minutes I too let the water soak me from head to toe. Then I knew we had to cap it off and decide what to do with it.

It seemed we had tapped into an underground river that nobody knew about. I had all the men from the valley helping me with the newly sprung well.

Together over the next few days we made furrows so the thirsty land would sap up the life-giving water. Before long, green plants began to appear and folks didn't have to make forays to the foothills for water.

I did not charge anybody for the use of the water; to me it was a gift from above. Within two months Harscrabble Valley was lush and green. Folks began to plant trees and they sprang to life on the valley floor.

All this time I still thought about Shasta and longed to see her once again.

Then one afternoon I was out near the pumps checking on the water when I saw a person on a horse coming closer and closer. At first I thought it might just be one of my neighbors checking on the water supply and planning on passing the time. Then the horse drew nearer and I stopped what I was doing as Shasta drew reins on her horse.

I ran to her and helped her down from the horse. If she had changed since going to Ohio it was for the better. She was lovelier than ever.

"I'm back," Shasta said. "Back where I belong. It is so good to see you, Horace. I missed you."

Then I told her how much I missed her and how it felt to see her once again.

After a while we spoke of the valley and what the well had done for it. She couldn't get over how beautiful the valley had become.

"It's a place I want to stay in the rest of my life," I said. "Me and the woman who would wed up with me."

It didn't take a slow-witted person to get my meaning. And Shasta was far from being slow-witted.

At that hour she accepted my offer of marriage.

A few months later we were wed in her ranch house which she had sold along with the property since the two of us would live on my ranch.

The new owner wanted Johnny Clover to run the place since he was a businessman from New York and rarely got away from the city.

In time Shasta had a book accepted and published. It was all about her growing up in Hardscrabble Valley.

She often asked me if there were any interesting adventures that had happened to me in the times of my travels.

I always told her I couldn't think of any.